STRANGER THINGS™

ZOMBIE BOYS

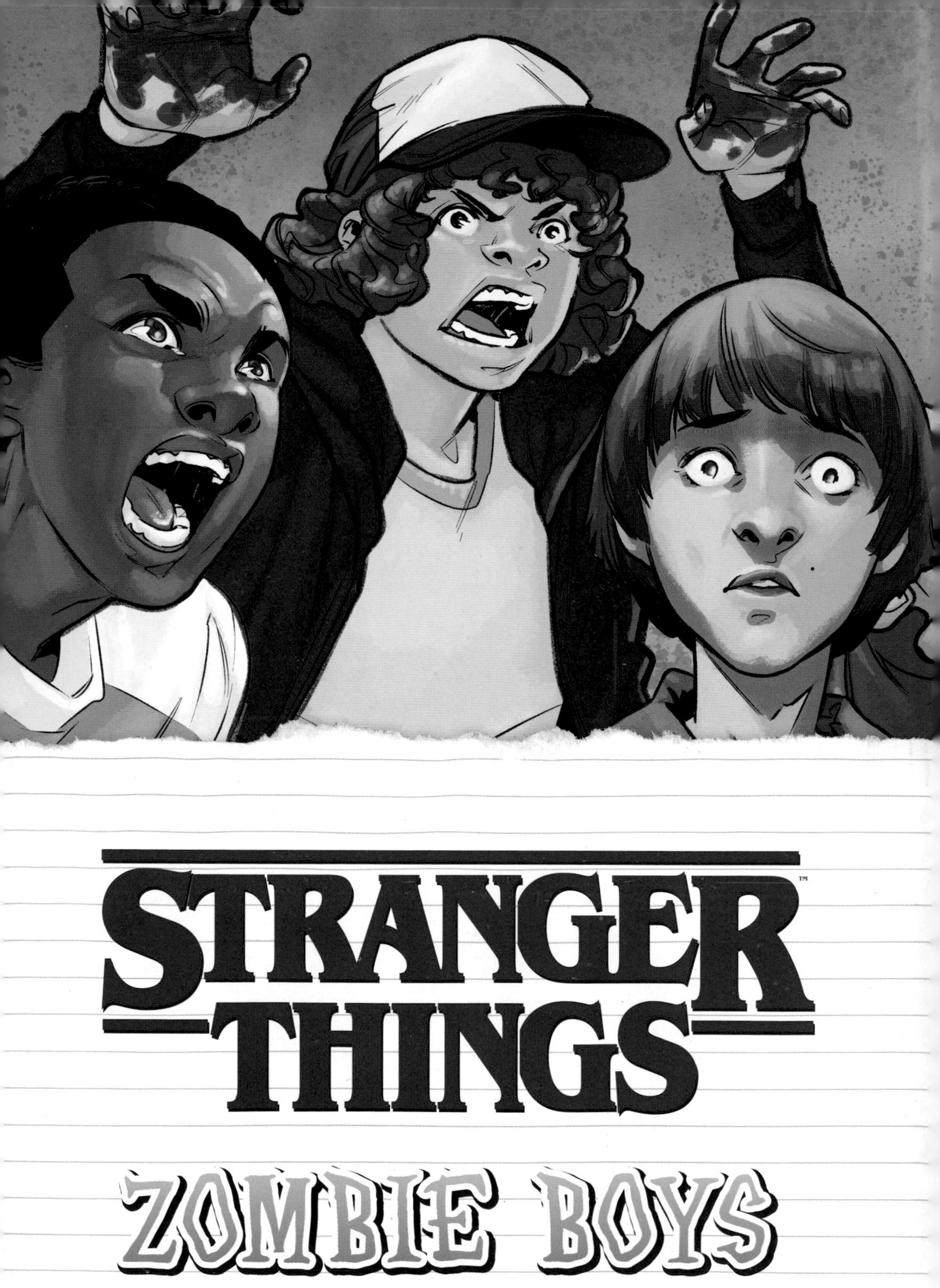

STRANGER THINGS™

ZOMBIE BOYS

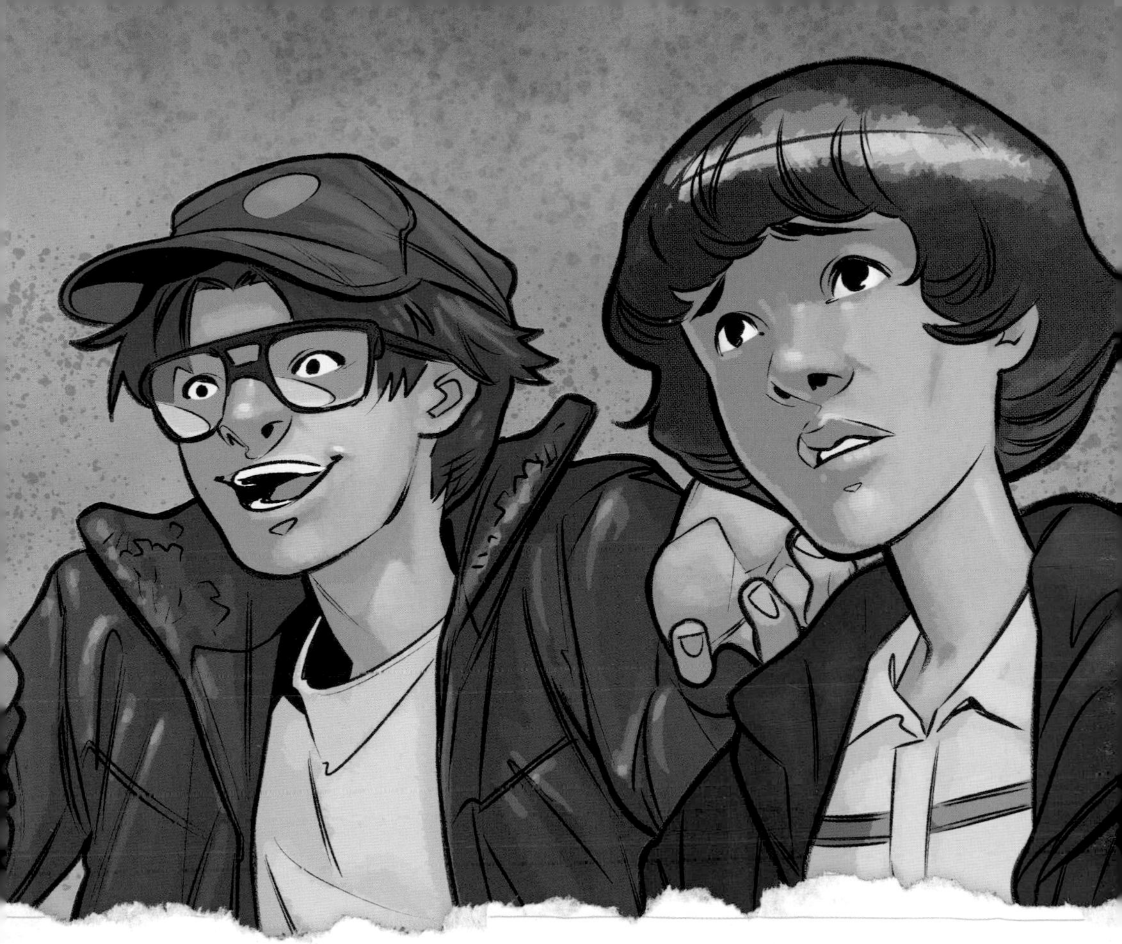

script by

GREG PAK

Art by

VALERIA FAVOCCIA

colors by

DAN JACKSON

Lettering by

NATE PIEKOS OF BLAMBOT®

cover Art by

RON CHAN

Dark Horse Books

President & Publisher
MIKE RICHARDSON

Editor
SPENCER CUSHING

Assistant Editor
KONNER KNUDSEN

Designer
PATRICK SATTERFIELD

Digital Art Technician
ALLYSON HALLER

Published by DARK HORSE BOOKS
A division of Dark Horse Comics LLC
10956 SE Main Street
Milwaukie, OR 97222

DarkHorse.com

First edition: February 2020
ISBN 978-1-50671-309-0

10 9 8 7 6 5 4 3 2
Printed in China

To find a comics shop in your area, visit comicshoplocator.com

Library of Congress Cataloging-in-Publication Data

Names: Pak, Greg, author. | Favoccia, Valeria, artist. | Jackson, Dan, 1971- colourist. | Piekos, Nate, letterer. | Chan, Ron, cover artist.
Title: Stranger Things : zombie boys / story by Greg Pak ; art by Valeria Favoccia ; colors by Dan Jackson ; lettering by Nate Piekos of Blambot ; cover art by Ron Chan.
Description: First edition. | Milwaukie, OR : Dark Horse Books, 2020. | Audience: Ages 12+ | Audience: Grades 4-6 | Summary: After defeating the Demogorgon, Mike, Lucas, Dustin, and Will struggle to adjust back to normal life, but just when their friendships begin to crack, new kid Joey Kim helps them come to terms with the supernatural horrors they experienced by making a zombie movie.
Identifiers: LCCN 2019042250 | ISBN 9781506713090 (paperback)
Subjects: LCSH: Graphic novels. | CYAC: Graphic novels. | Supernatural--Fiction. | Friendship--Fiction. | Motion pictures--Production and direction--Fiction. | Video recordings--Fiction. | Horror films--Fiction.
Classification: LCC PZ7.7.P16 St 2020 | DDC 741.5/973--dc23
LC record available at https://lccn.loc.gov/2019042250

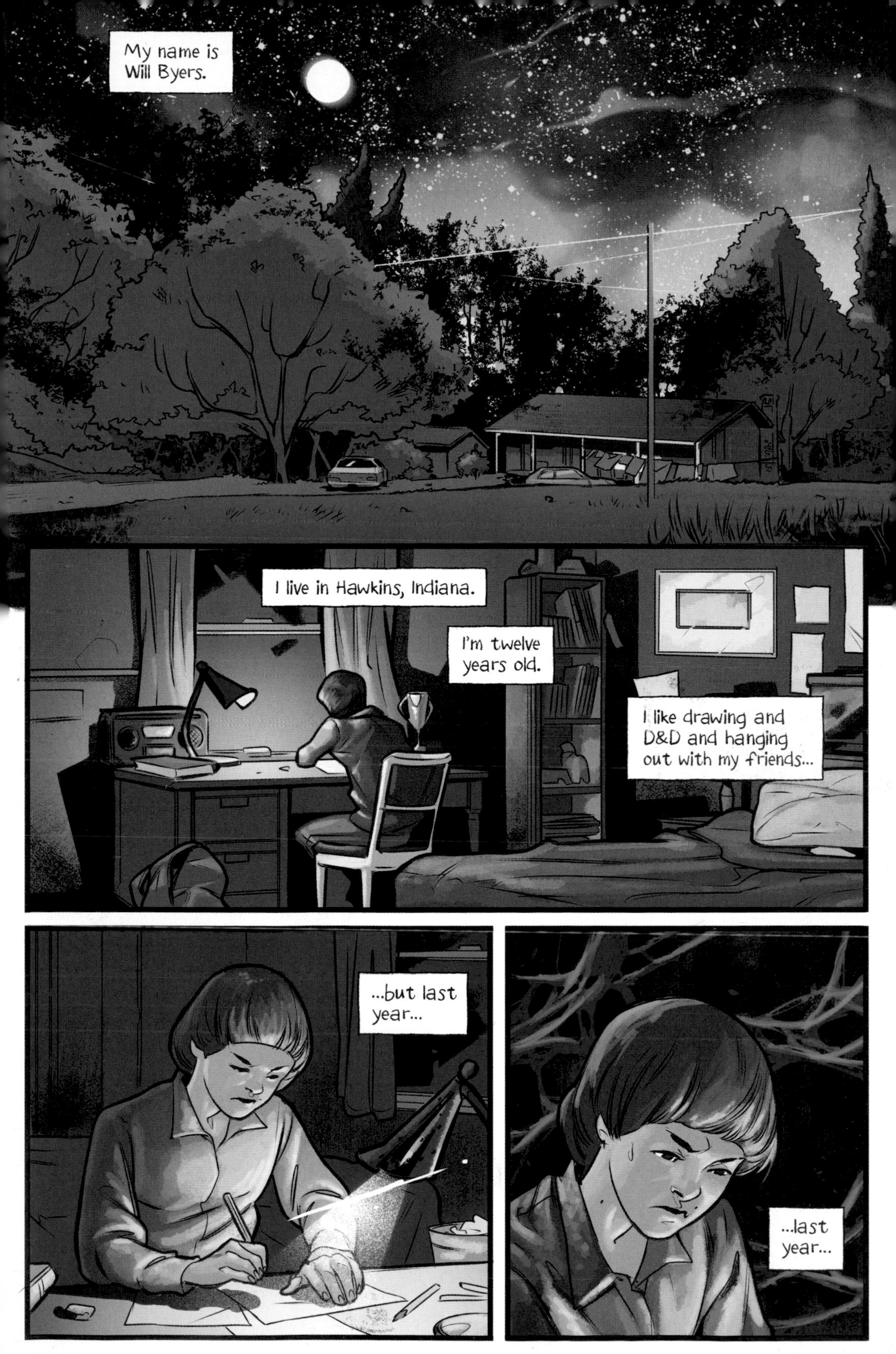
My name is Will Byers.
I live in Hawkins, Indiana.
I'm twelve years old.
I like drawing and D&D and hanging out with my friends...
...but last year...
...last year...

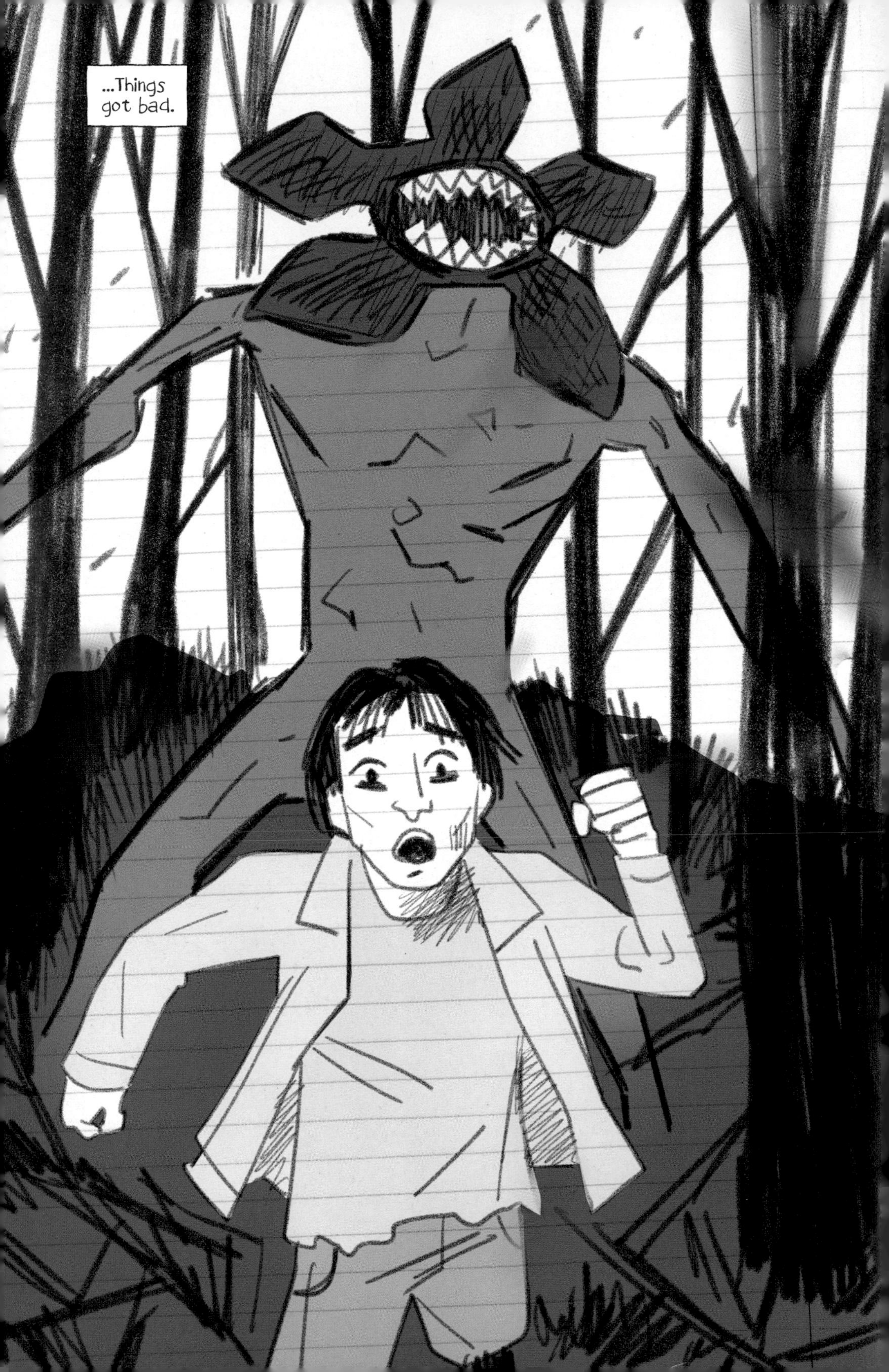
...Things got bad.

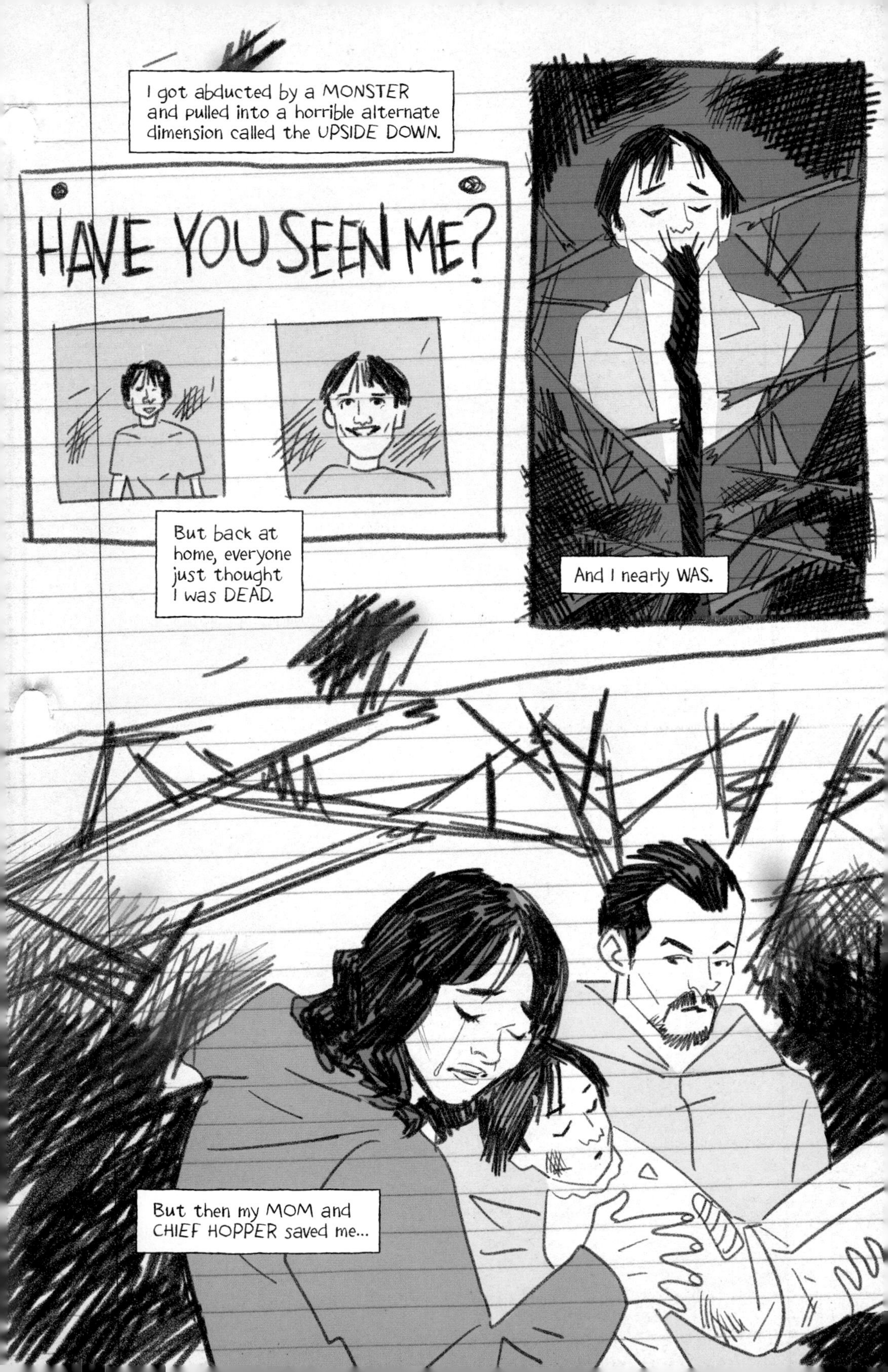
I got abducted by a MONSTER and pulled into a horrible alternate dimension called the UPSIDE DOWN.
HAVE YOU SEEN ME?
But back at home, everyone just thought I was DEAD.
And I nearly WAS.
But then my MOM and CHIEF HOPPER saved me...

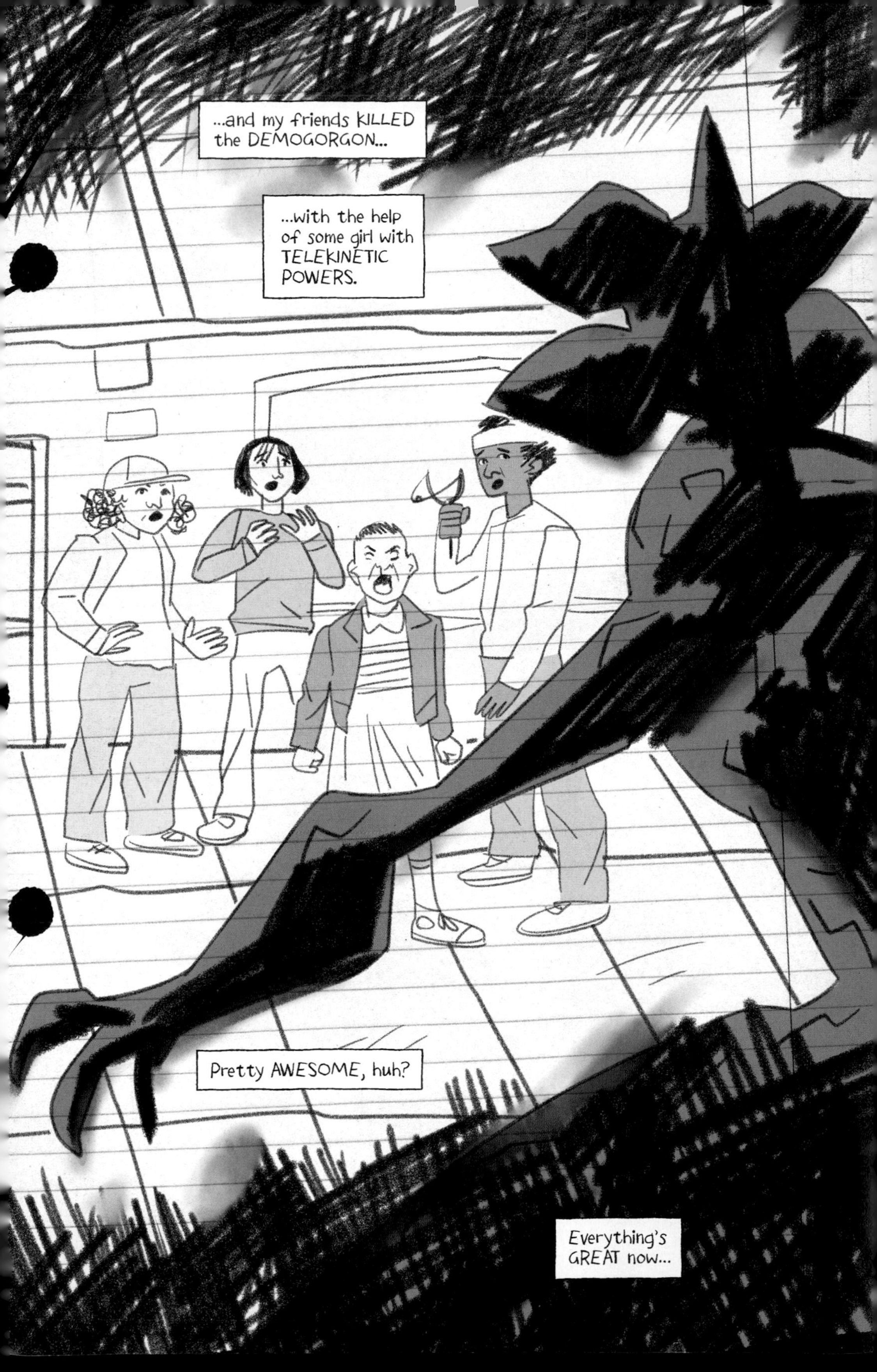

...and my friends KILLED the DEMOGORGON...
...with the help of some girl with TELEKINETIC POWERS.
Pretty AWESOME, huh?
Everything's GREAT now...

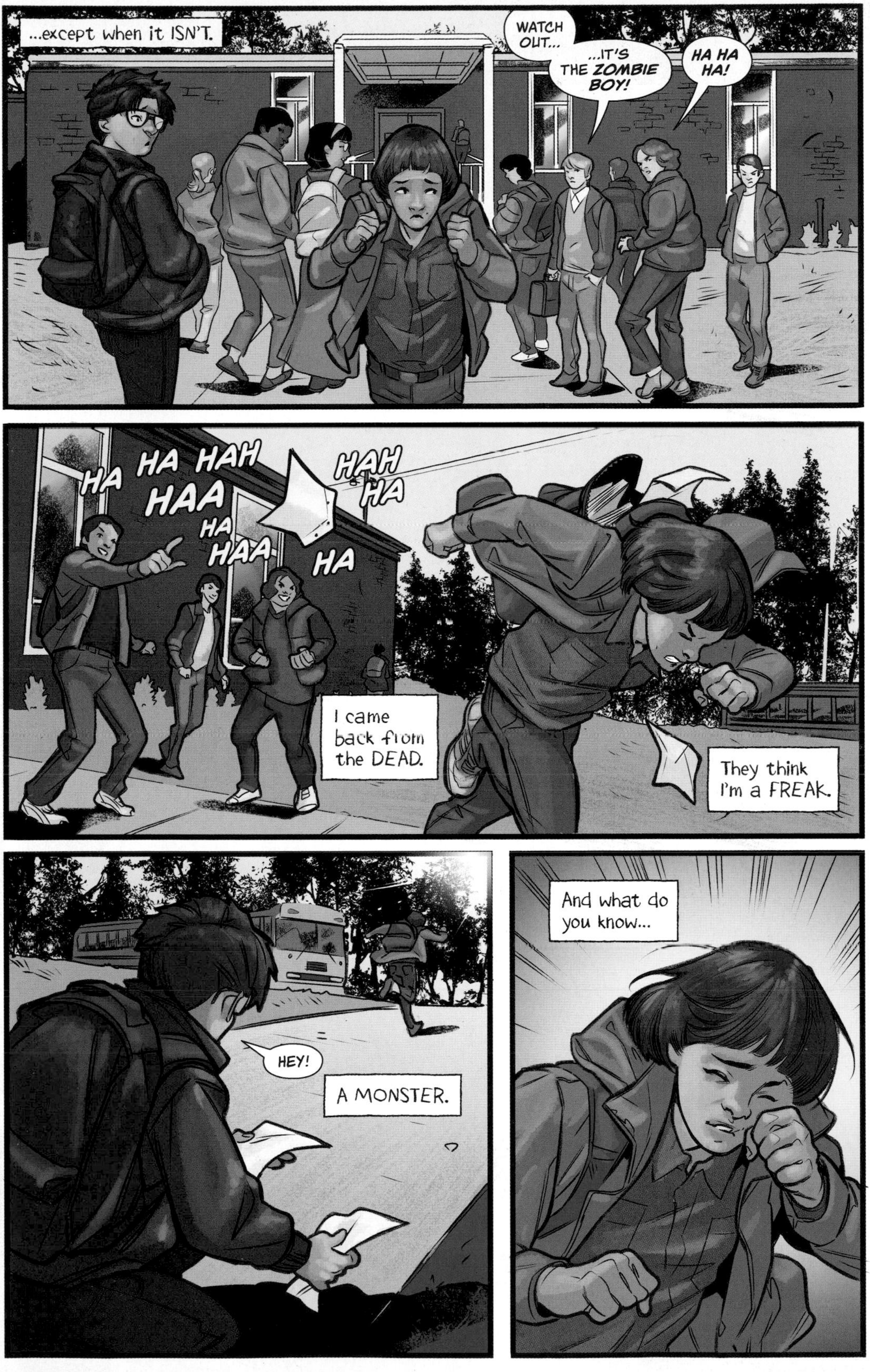
...except when it ISN'T.
WATCH OUT...
...IT'S THE ZOMBIE BOY!
HA HA HA!
HA HA HAH
HAA
HA
HAA
HAH
HA
HA
I came back from the DEAD.
They think I'm a FREAK.
HEY!
A MONSTER.
And what do you know...

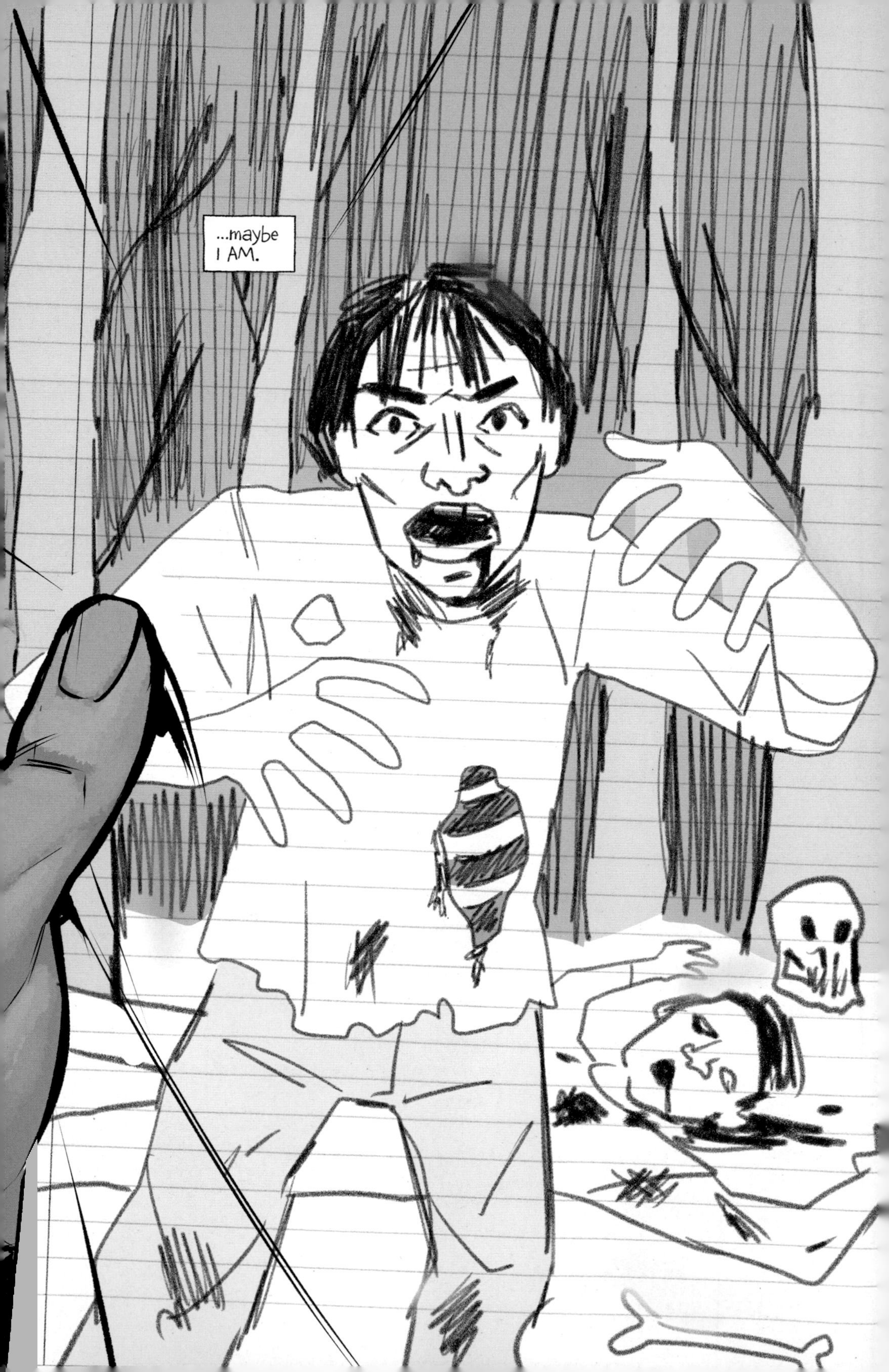
...maybe
I AM.

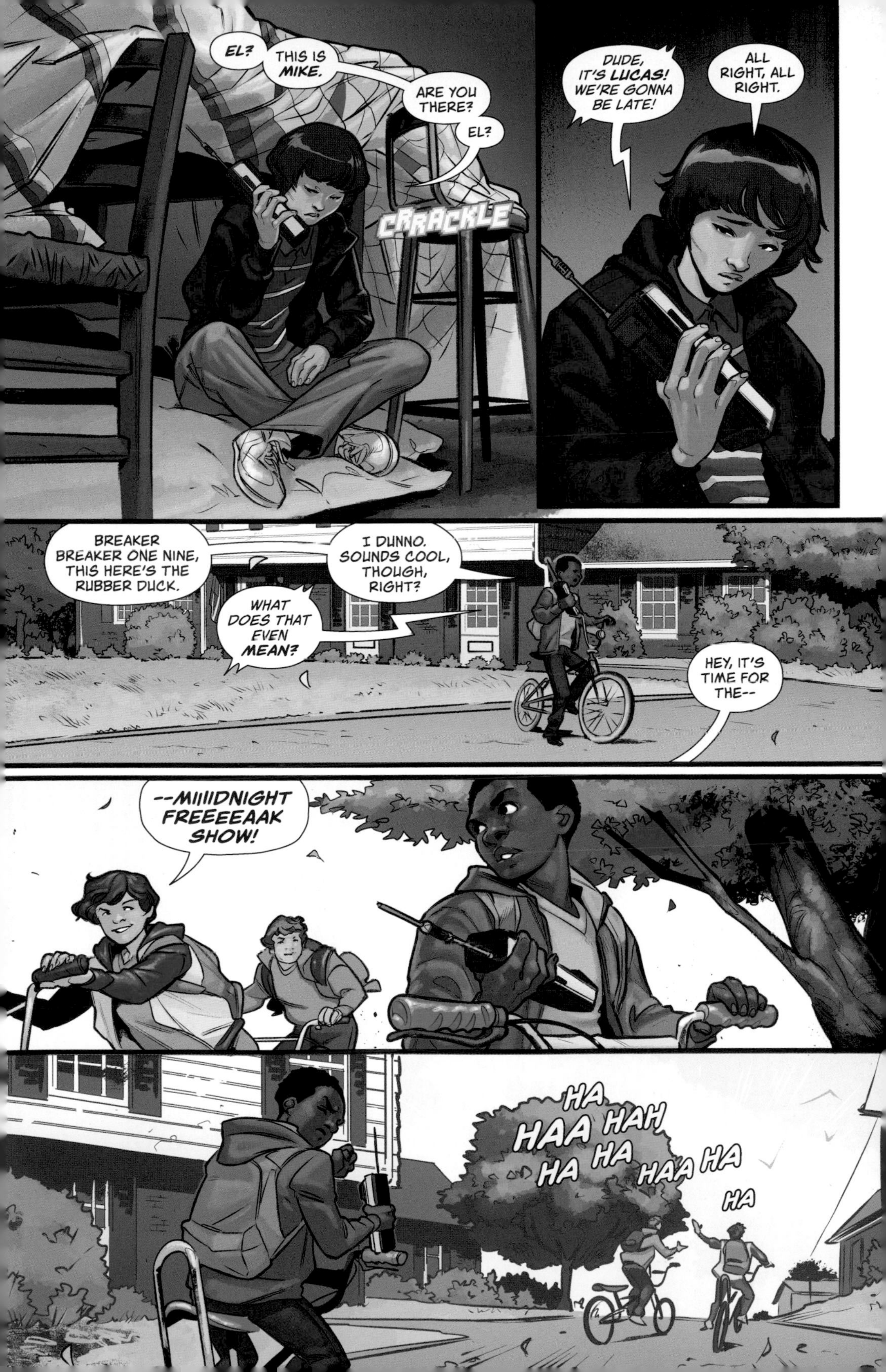
EL?
THIS IS MIKE.
ARE YOU THERE?
EL?
CRRACKLE
DUDE, IT'S LUCAS! WE'RE GONNA BE LATE!
ALL RIGHT, ALL RIGHT.
BREAKER BREAKER ONE NINE, THIS HERE'S THE RUBBER DUCK.
WHAT DOES THAT EVEN MEAN?
I DUNNO. SOUNDS COOL, THOUGH, RIGHT?
HEY, IT'S TIME FOR THE--
--MIIIIDNIGHT FREEEEAAK SHOW!
HA
HAA HAH
HA HA
HAA HA
HA

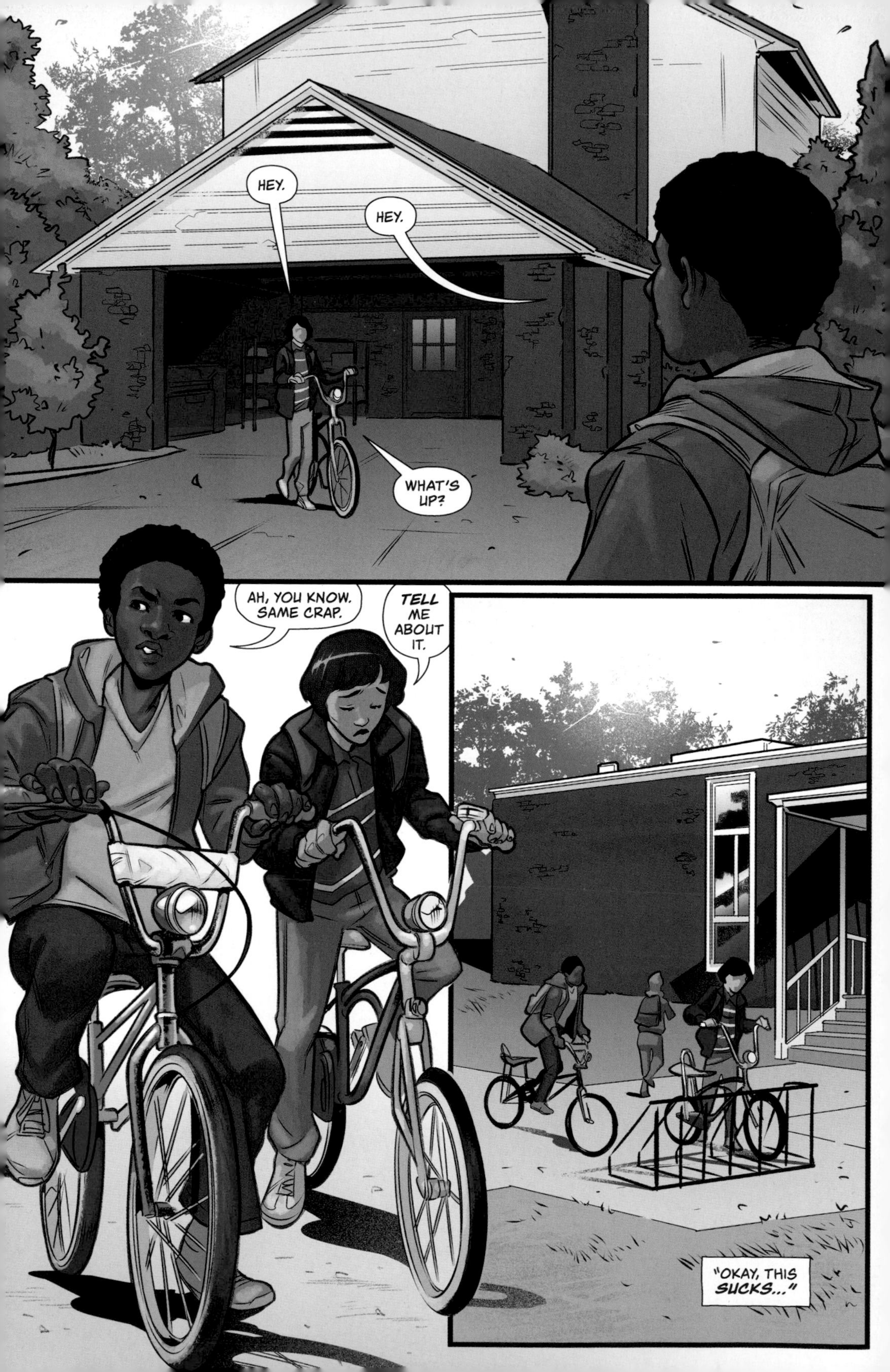
HEY.
HEY.
WHAT'S UP?
AH, YOU KNOW. SAME CRAP.
TELL ME ABOUT IT.
"OKAY, THIS SUCKS..."

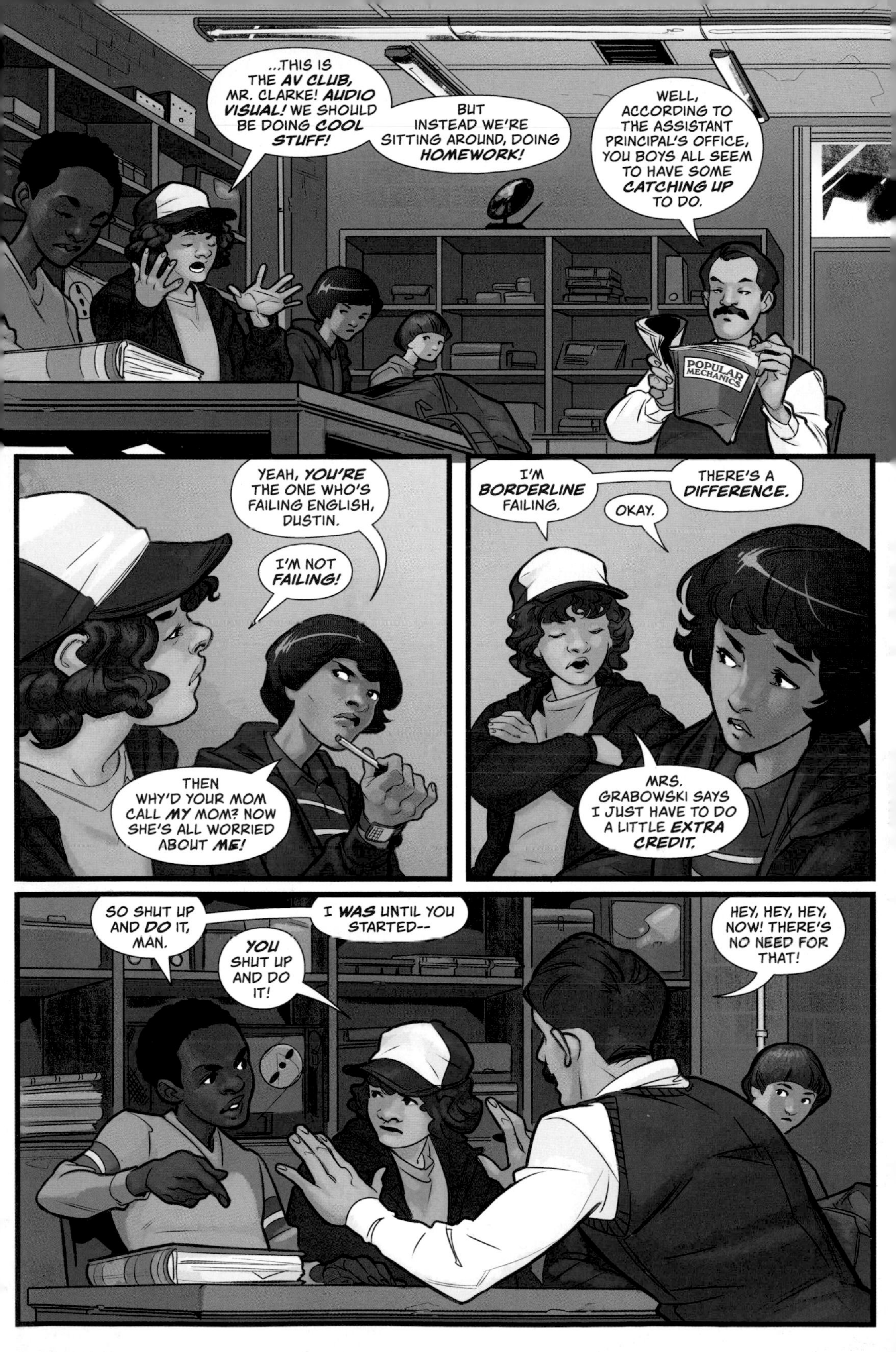
...THIS IS THE AV CLUB, MR. CLARKE! AUDIO VISUAL! WE SHOULD BE DOING COOL STUFF!
BUT INSTEAD WE'RE SITTING AROUND, DOING HOMEWORK!
WELL, ACCORDING TO THE ASSISTANT PRINCIPAL'S OFFICE, YOU BOYS ALL SEEM TO HAVE SOME CATCHING UP TO DO.
POPULAR MECHANICS
YEAH, YOU'RE THE ONE WHO'S FAILING ENGLISH, DUSTIN.
I'M NOT FAILING!
THEN WHY'D YOUR MOM CALL MY MOM? NOW SHE'S ALL WORRIED ABOUT ME!
I'M BORDERLINE FAILING.
THERE'S A DIFFERENCE.
OKAY.
MRS. GRABOWSKI SAYS I JUST HAVE TO DO A LITTLE EXTRA CREDIT.
SO SHUT UP AND DO IT, MAN.
I WAS UNTIL YOU STARTED--
YOU SHUT UP AND DO IT!
HEY, HEY, HEY, NOW! THERE'S NO NEED FOR THAT!

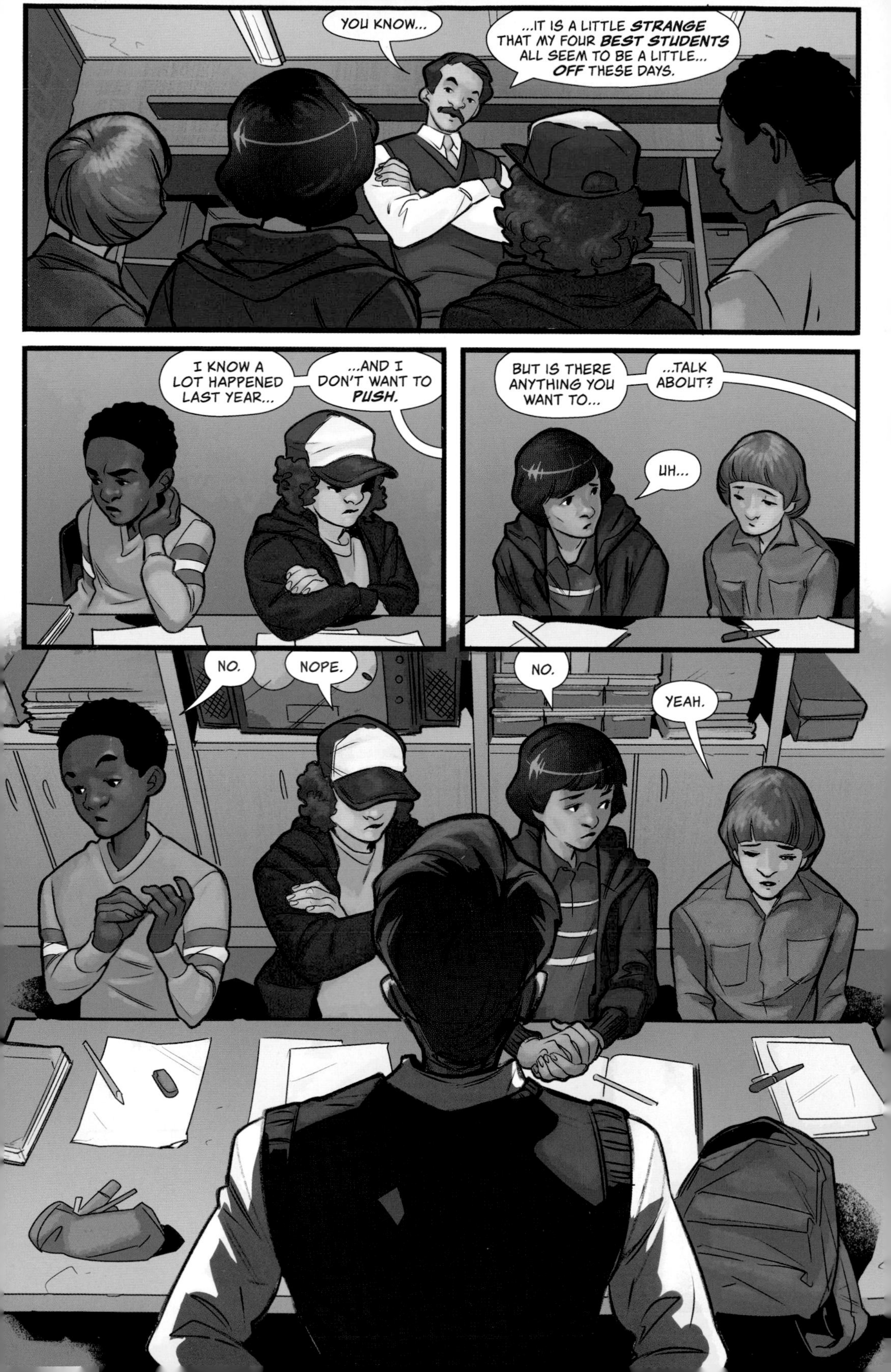

YOU KNOW...
...IT IS A LITTLE STRANGE THAT MY FOUR BEST STUDENTS ALL SEEM TO BE A LITTLE... OFF THESE DAYS.
I KNOW A LOT HAPPENED LAST YEAR...
...AND I DON'T WANT TO PUSH.
BUT IS THERE ANYTHING YOU WANT TO...
...TALK ABOUT?
UH...
NO.
NOPE.
NO.
YEAH.

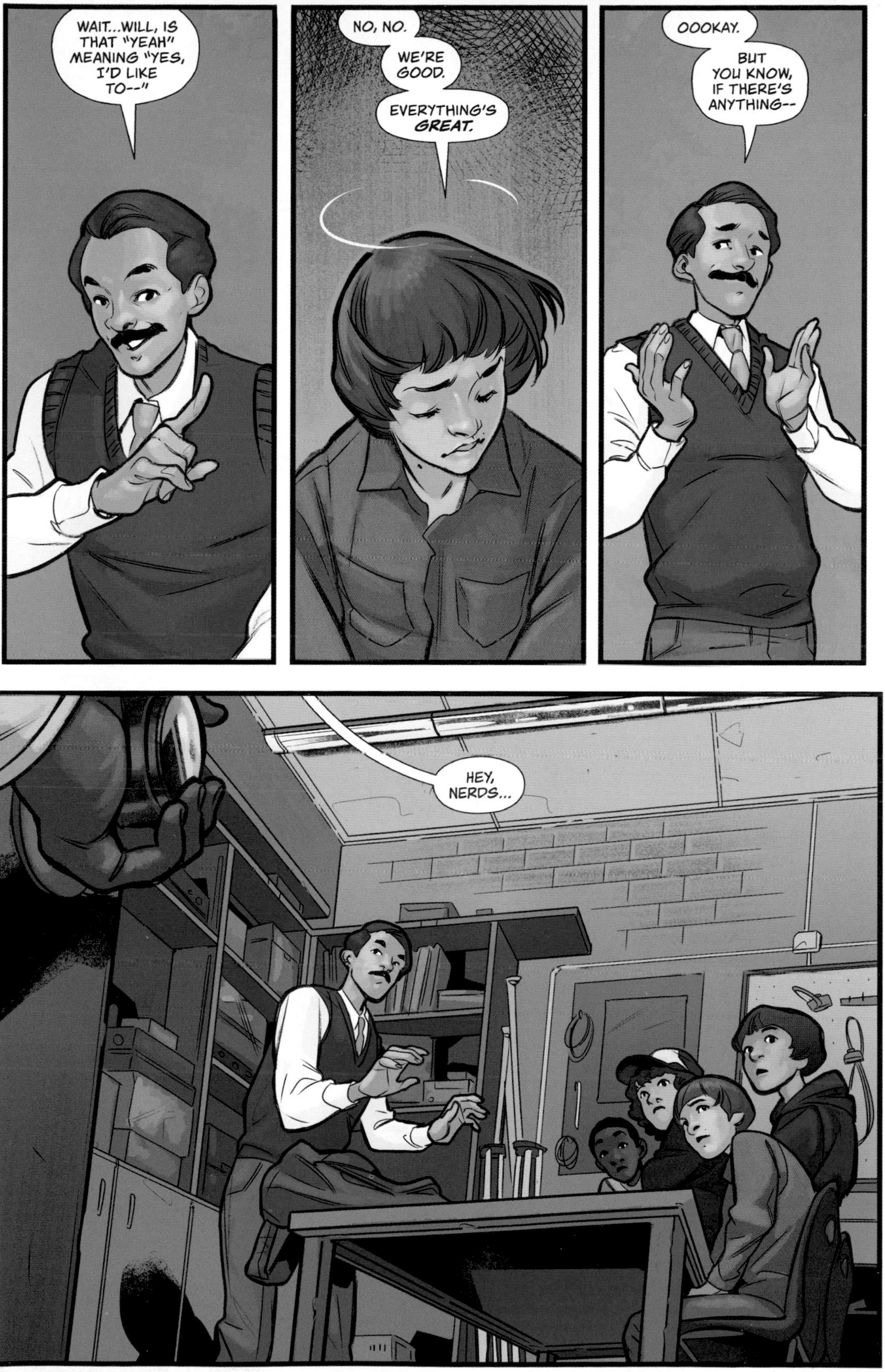
WAIT...WILL, IS THAT "YEAH" MEANING "YES, I'D LIKE TO--"
NO, NO.
WE'RE GOOD.
EVERYTHING'S **GREAT.**
OOOKAY.
BUT YOU KNOW, IF THERE'S ANYTHING--
HEY, NERDS...

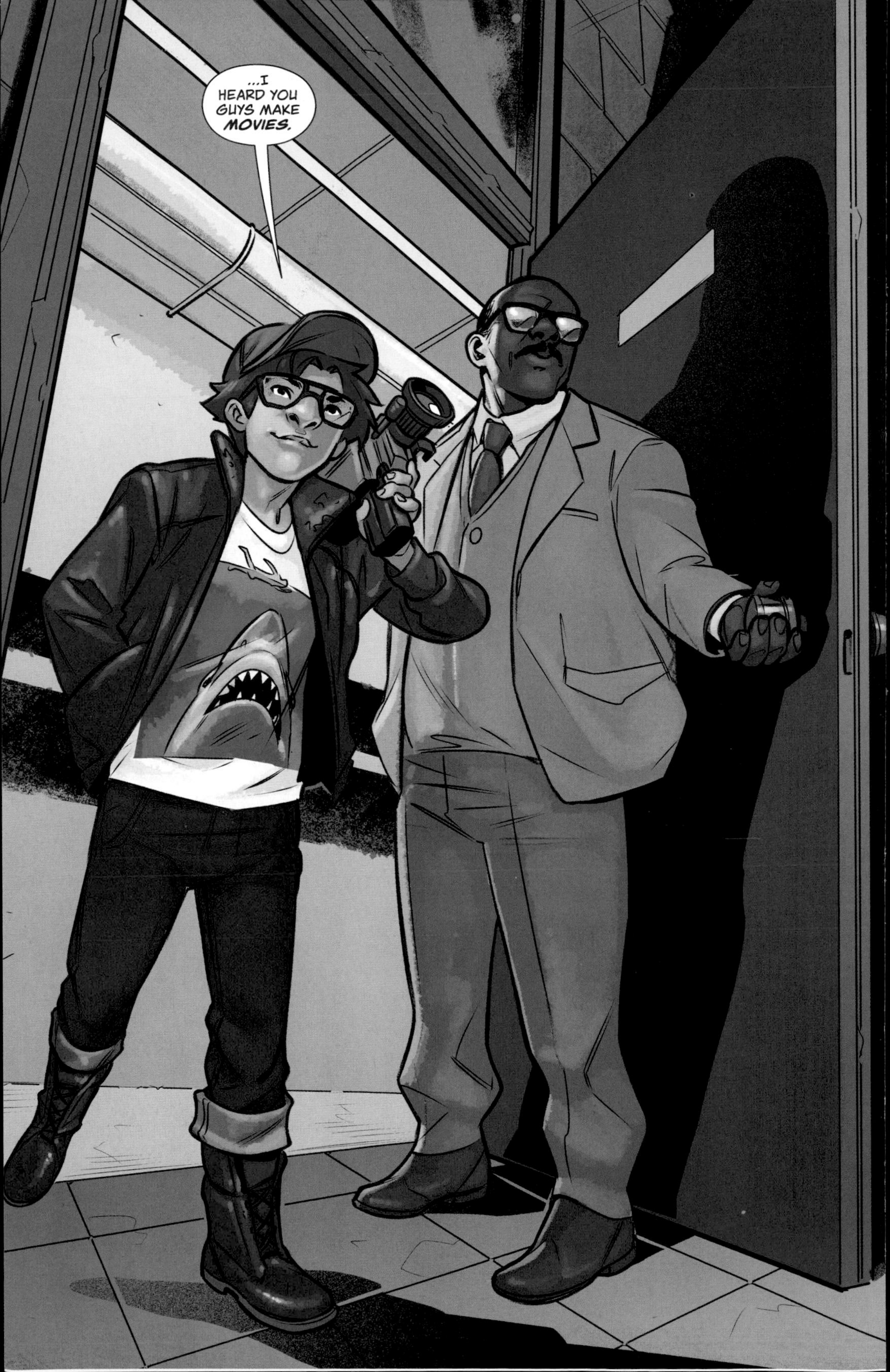
...I HEARD YOU GUYS MAKE *MOVIES.*

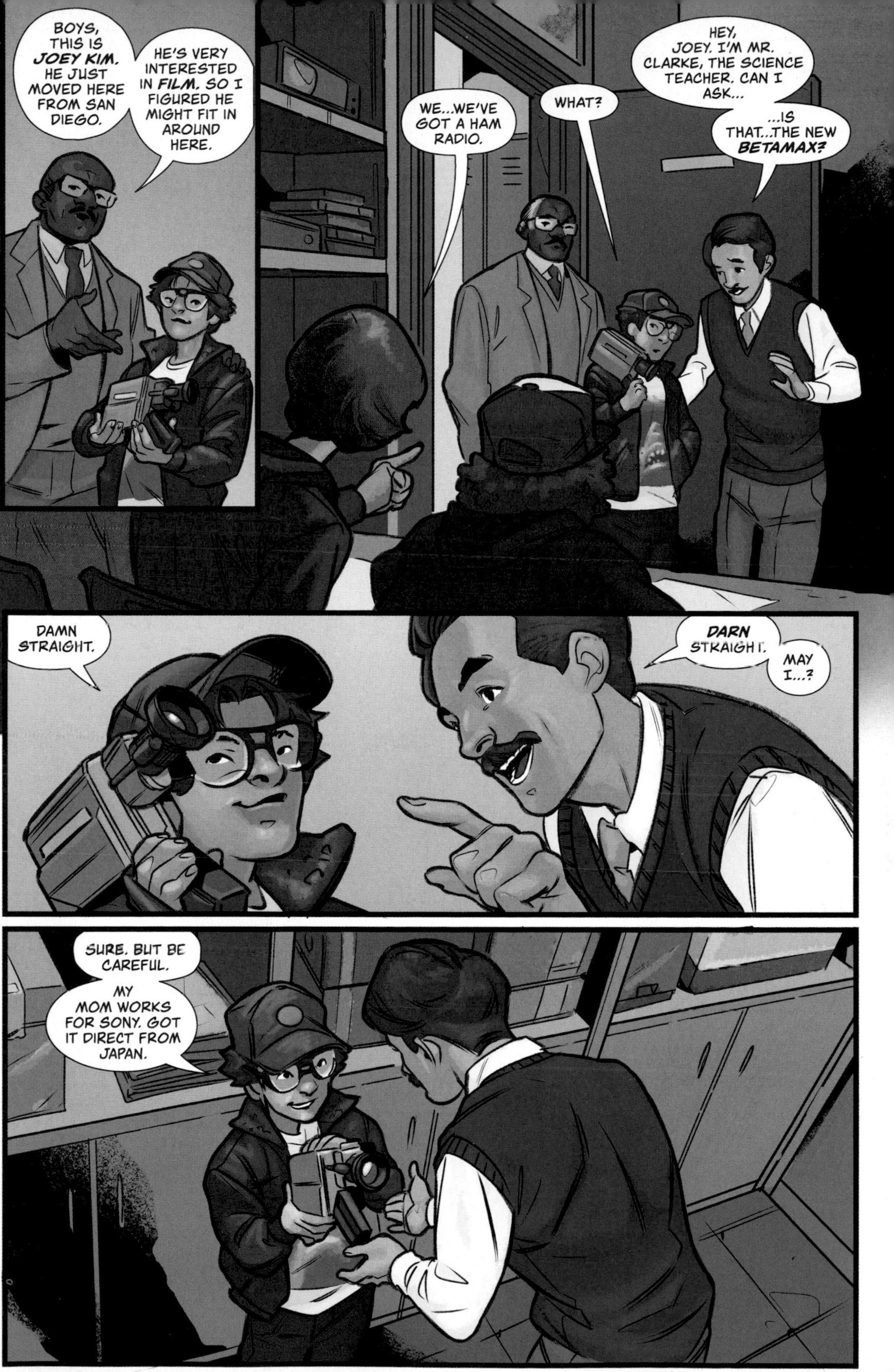

BOYS, THIS IS JOEY KIM. HE JUST MOVED HERE FROM SAN DIEGO.
HE'S VERY INTERESTED IN FILM. SO I FIGURED HE MIGHT FIT IN AROUND HERE.
WE...WE'VE GOT A HAM RADIO.
WHAT?
HEY, JOEY. I'M MR. CLARKE, THE SCIENCE TEACHER. CAN I ASK...
...IS THAT...THE NEW BETAMAX?
DAMN STRAIGHT.
DARN STRAIGHT.
MAY I...?
SURE. BUT BE CAREFUL.
MY MOM WORKS FOR SONY. GOT IT DIRECT FROM JAPAN.

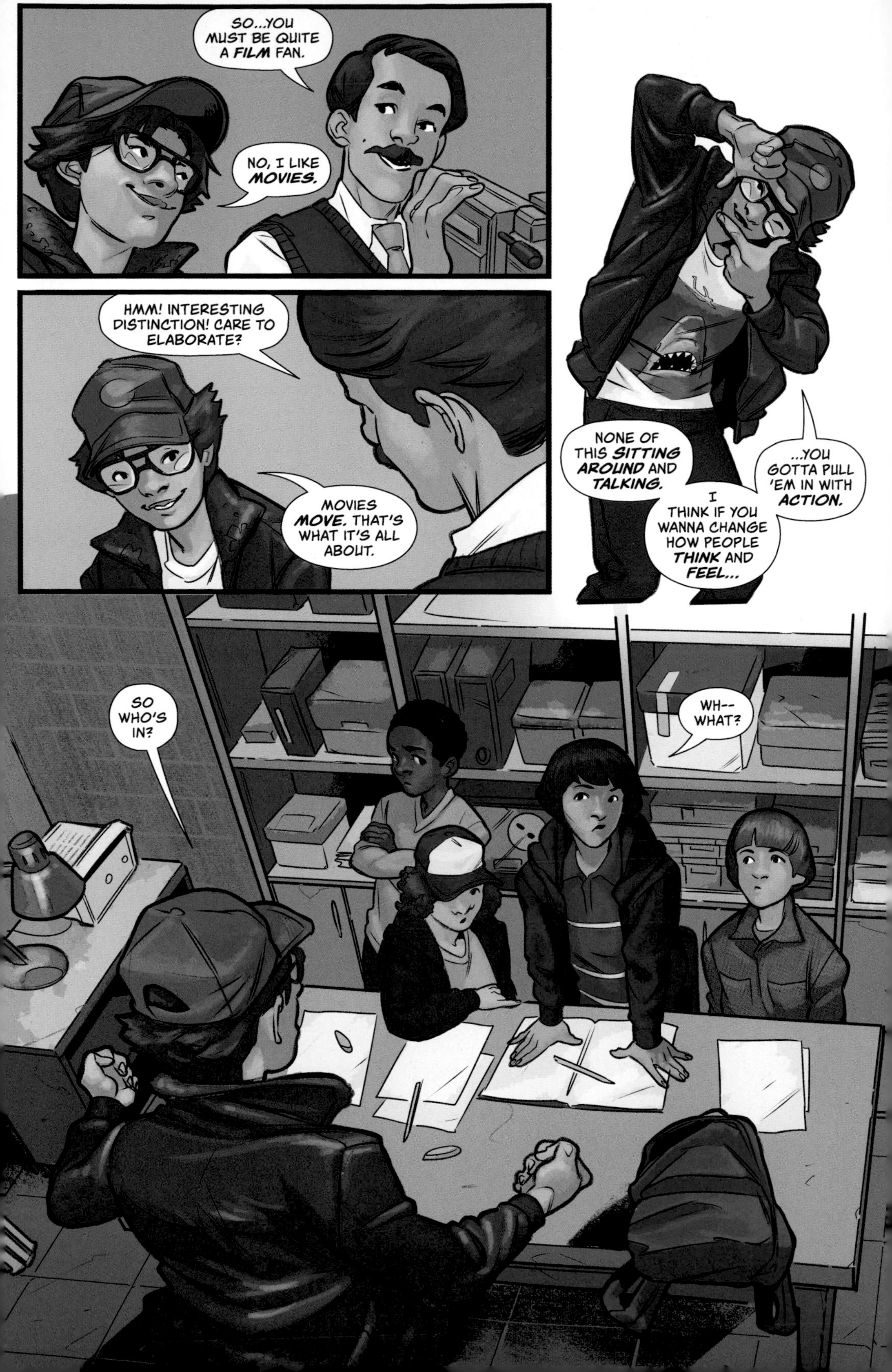
SO...YOU MUST BE QUITE A FILM FAN.
NO, I LIKE MOVIES.
HMM! INTERESTING DISTINCTION! CARE TO ELABORATE?
MOVIES MOVE. THAT'S WHAT IT'S ALL ABOUT.
NONE OF THIS SITTING AROUND AND TALKING.
I THINK IF YOU WANNA CHANGE HOW PEOPLE THINK AND FEEL...
...YOU GOTTA PULL 'EM IN WITH ACTION.
SO WHO'S IN?
WH-- WHAT?

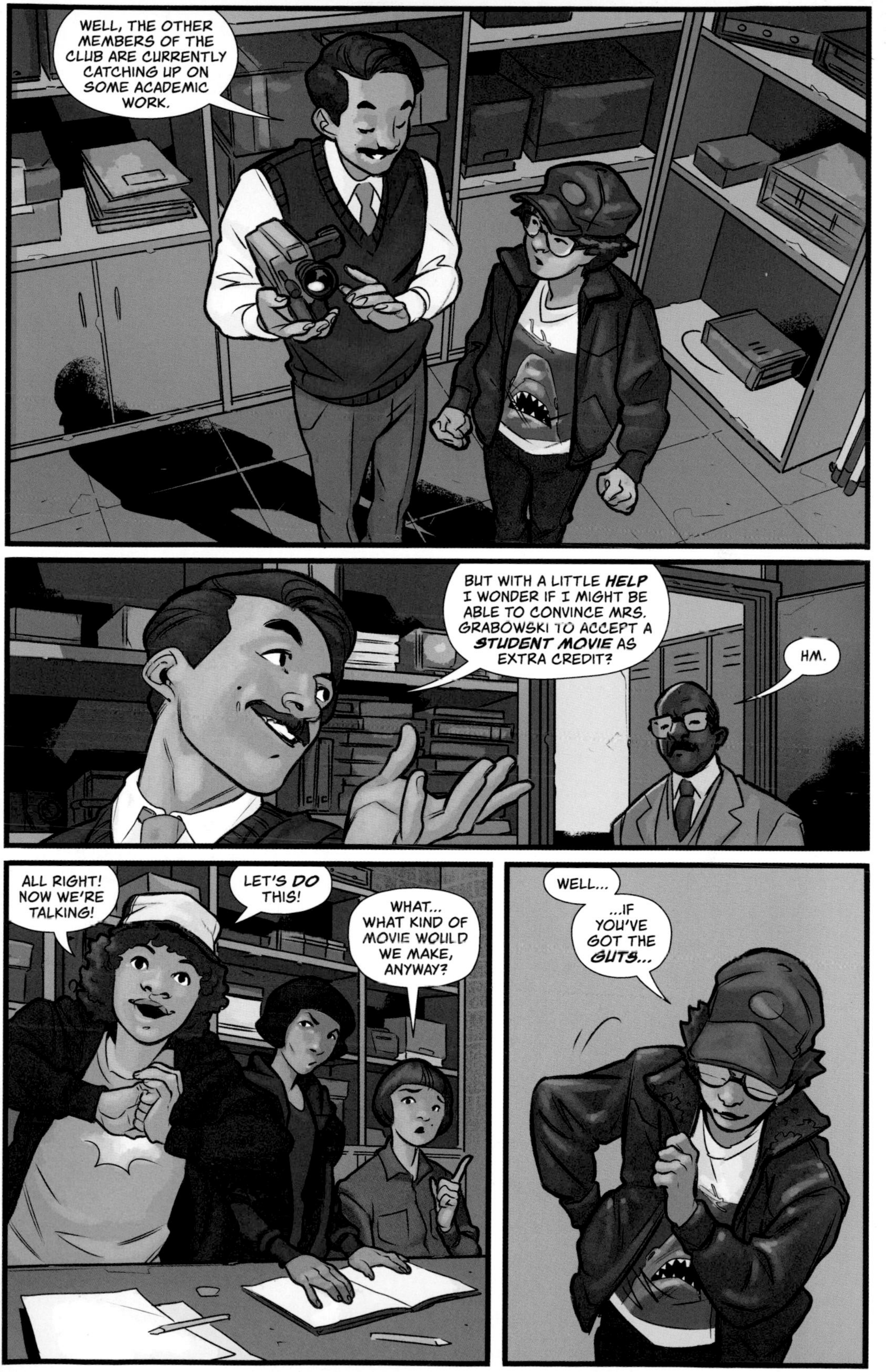
WELL, THE OTHER MEMBERS OF THE CLUB ARE CURRENTLY CATCHING UP ON SOME ACADEMIC WORK.
BUT WITH A LITTLE HELP I WONDER IF I MIGHT BE ABLE TO CONVINCE MRS. GRABOWSKI TO ACCEPT A STUDENT MOVIE AS EXTRA CREDIT?
HM.
ALL RIGHT! NOW WE'RE TALKING!
LET'S DO THIS!
WHAT... WHAT KIND OF MOVIE WOULD WE MAKE, ANYWAY?
WELL...
...IF YOU'VE GOT THE GUTS...

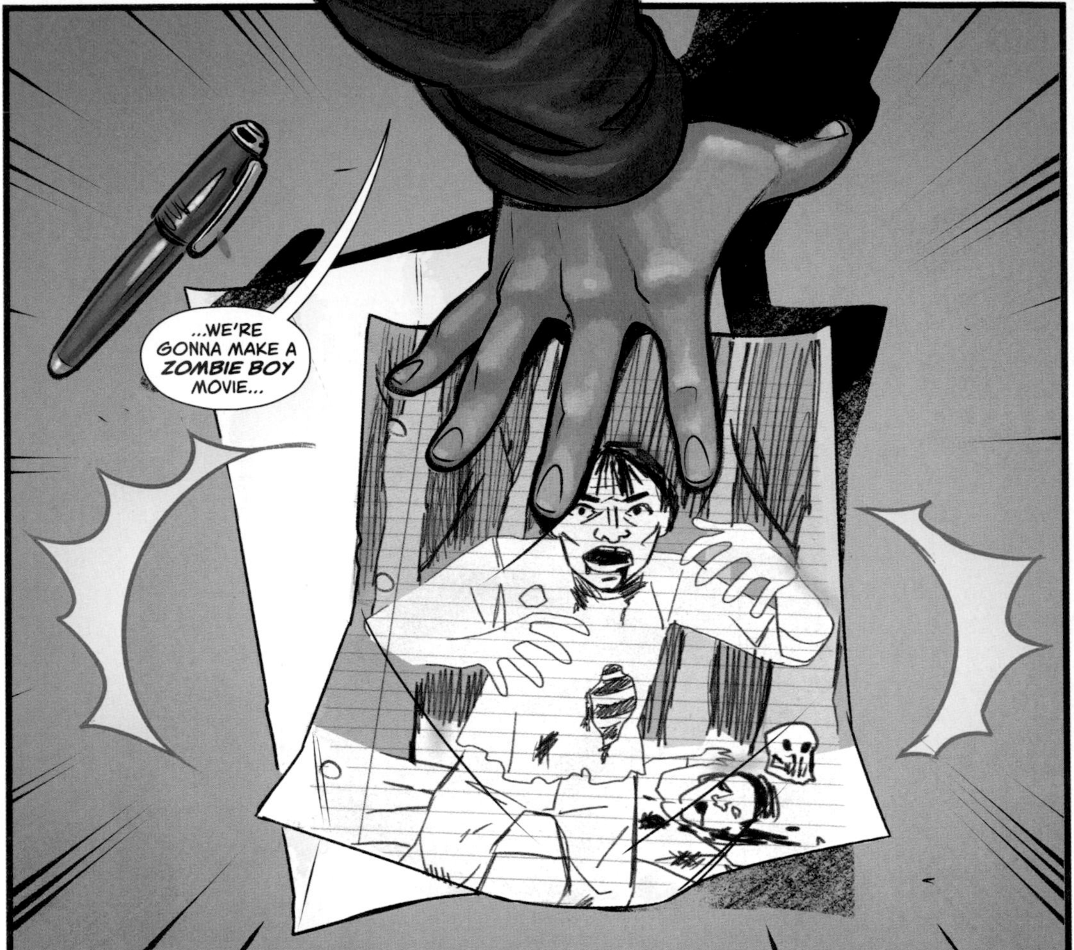
...WE'RE GONNA MAKE A ZOMBIE BOY MOVIE...

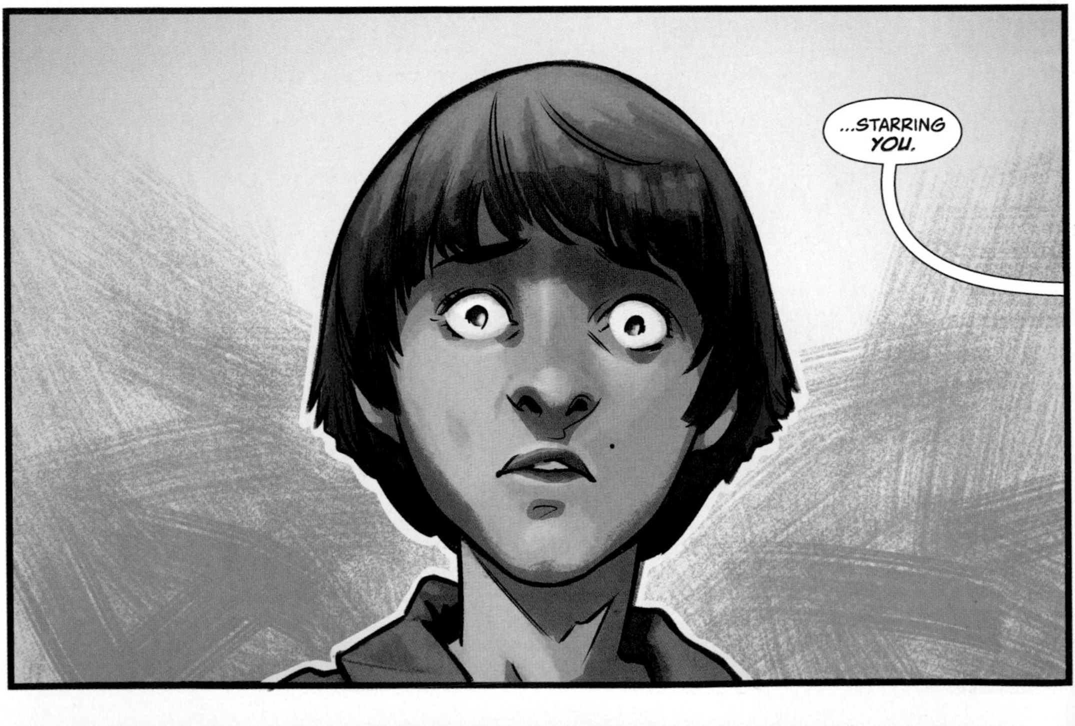
...STARRING YOU.

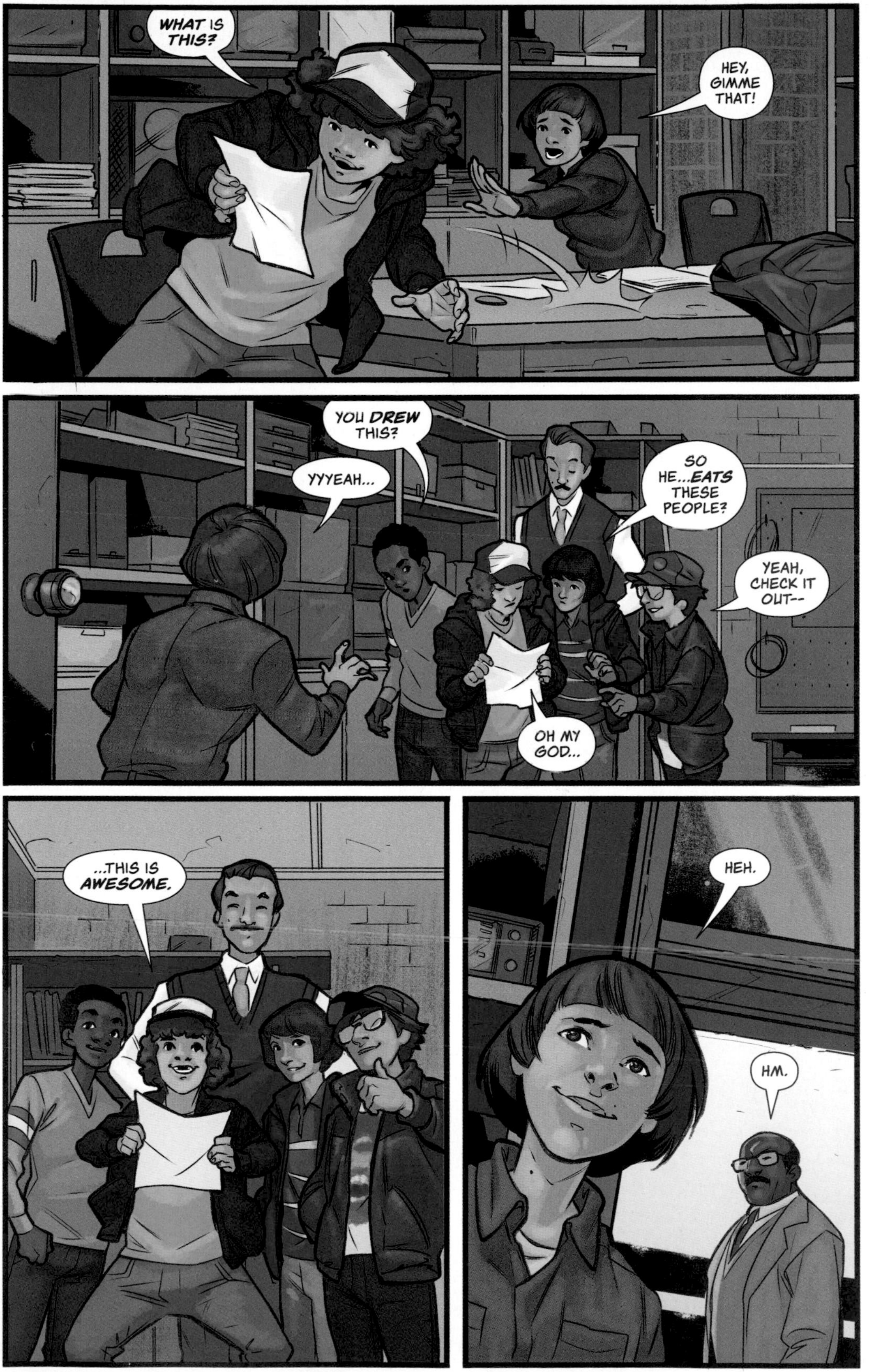
WHAT IS THIS?
HEY, GIMME THAT!
YOU DREW THIS?
YYYEAH...
SO HE...EATS THESE PEOPLE?
YEAH, CHECK IT OUT--
OH MY GOD...
...THIS IS AWESOME.
HEH.
HM.

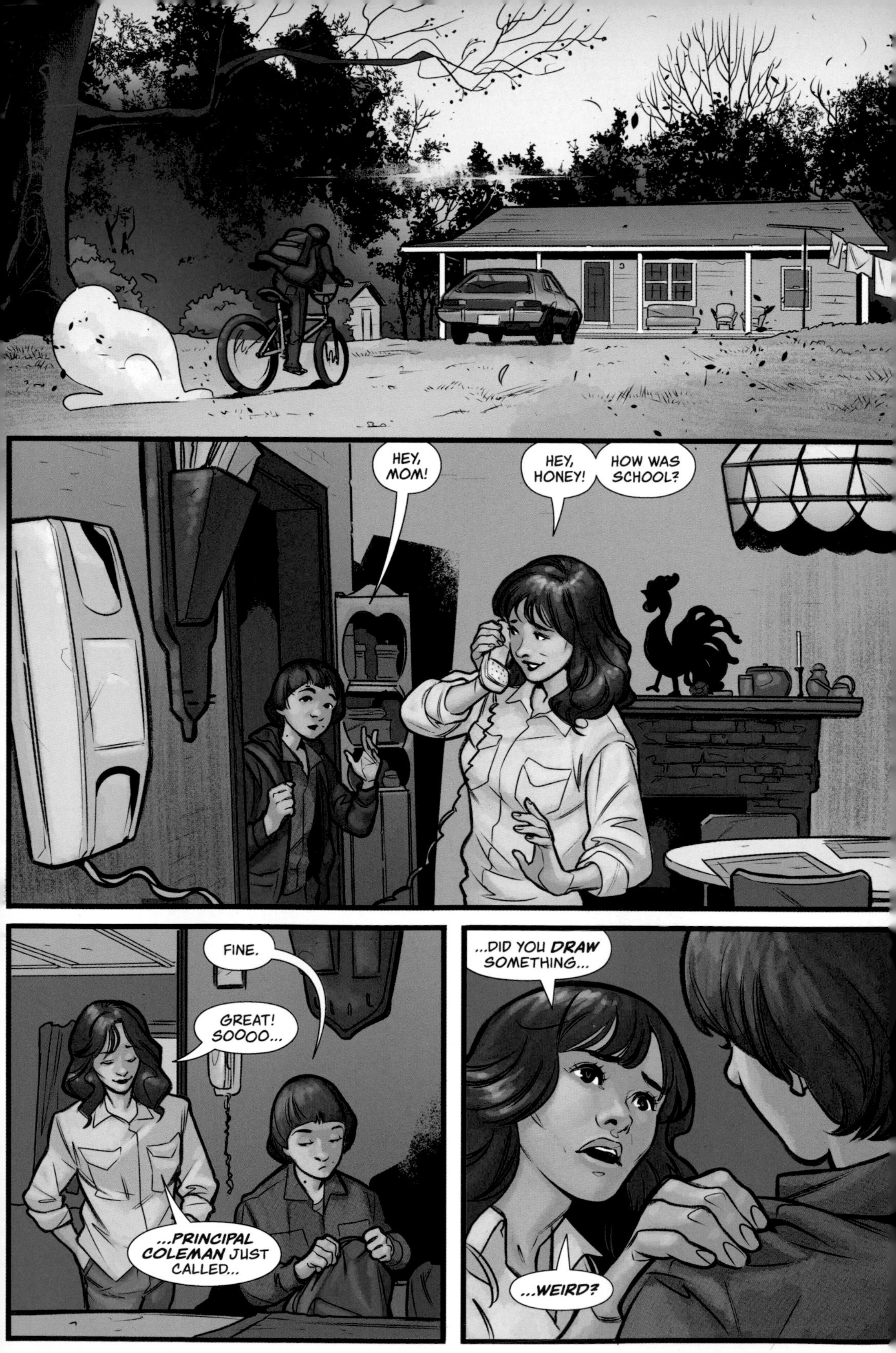
HEY, MOM!
HEY, HONEY!
HOW WAS SCHOOL?
FINE.
GREAT! SOOOO...
...PRINCIPAL COLEMAN JUST CALLED...
...DID YOU DRAW SOMETHING...
...WEIRD?

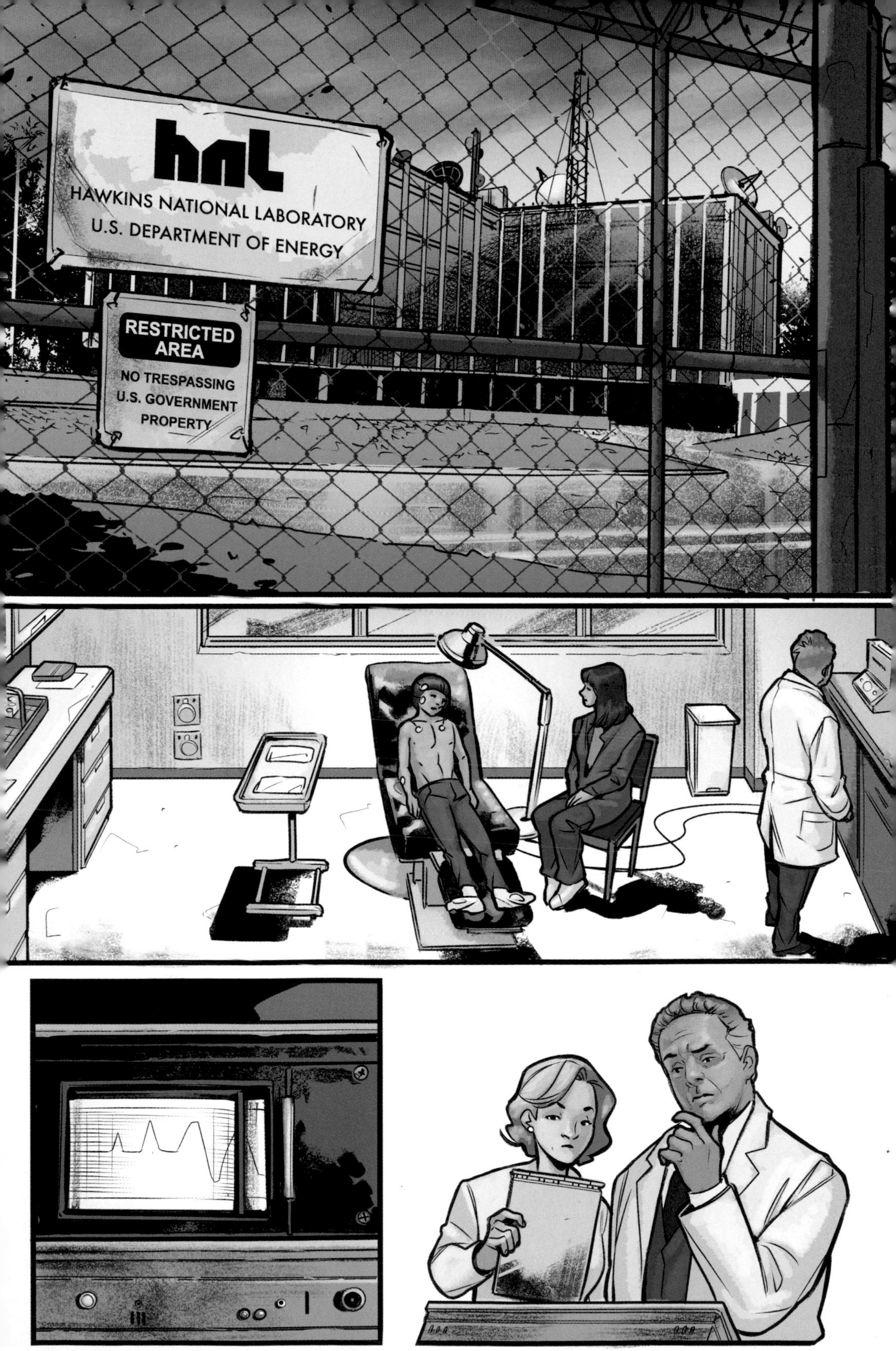
hnl
HAWKINS NATIONAL LABORATORY
U.S. DEPARTMENT OF ENERGY
RESTRICTED AREA
NO TRESPASSING
U.S. GOVERNMENT PROPERTY

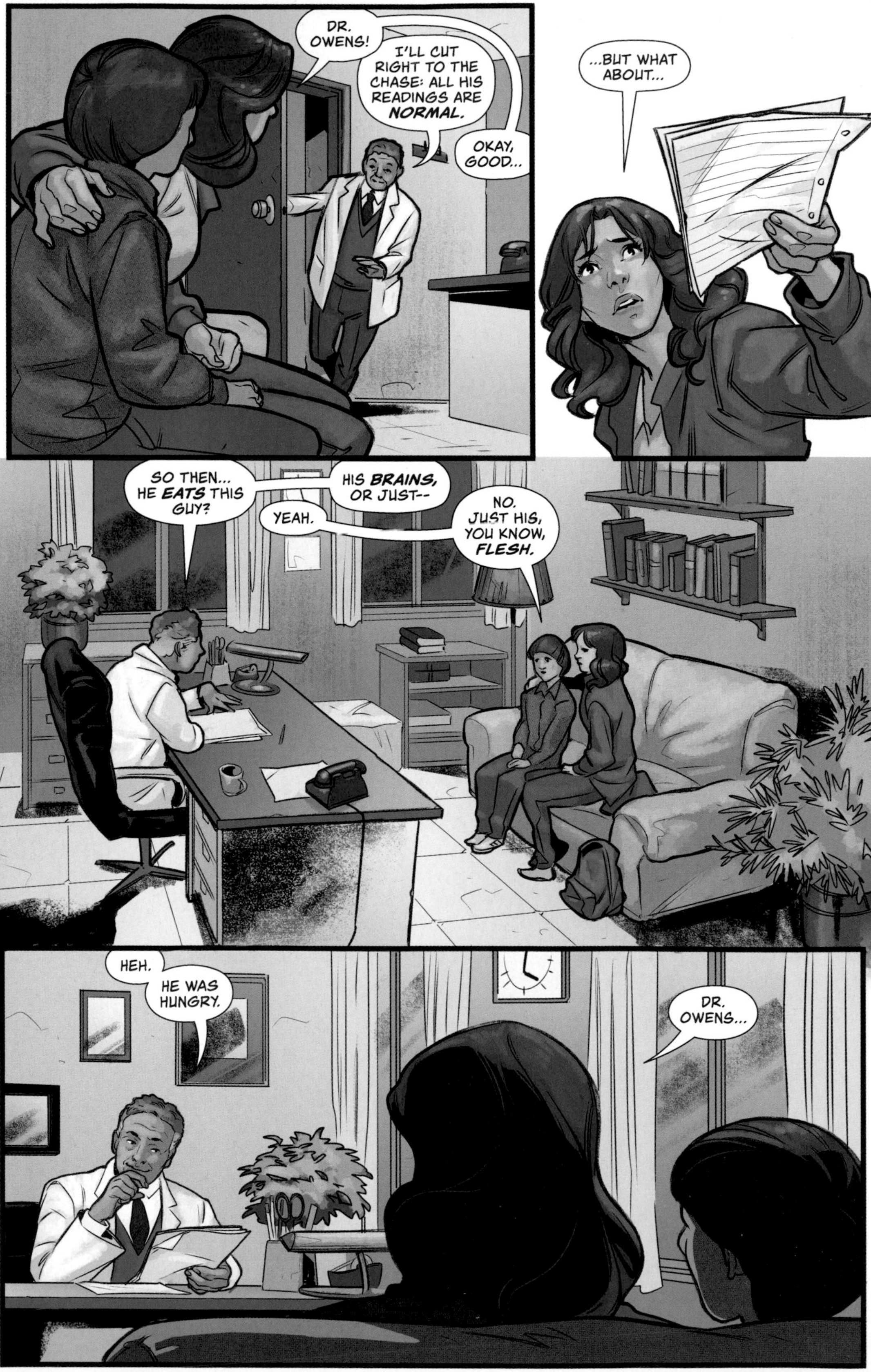
DR. OWENS!
I'LL CUT RIGHT TO THE CHASE: ALL HIS READINGS ARE **NORMAL.**
OKAY, GOOD...
...BUT WHAT ABOUT...
SO THEN... HE **EATS** THIS GUY?
YEAH.
HIS **BRAINS,** OR JUST--
NO. JUST HIS, YOU KNOW, **FLESH.**
HEH.
HE WAS HUNGRY.
DR. OWENS...

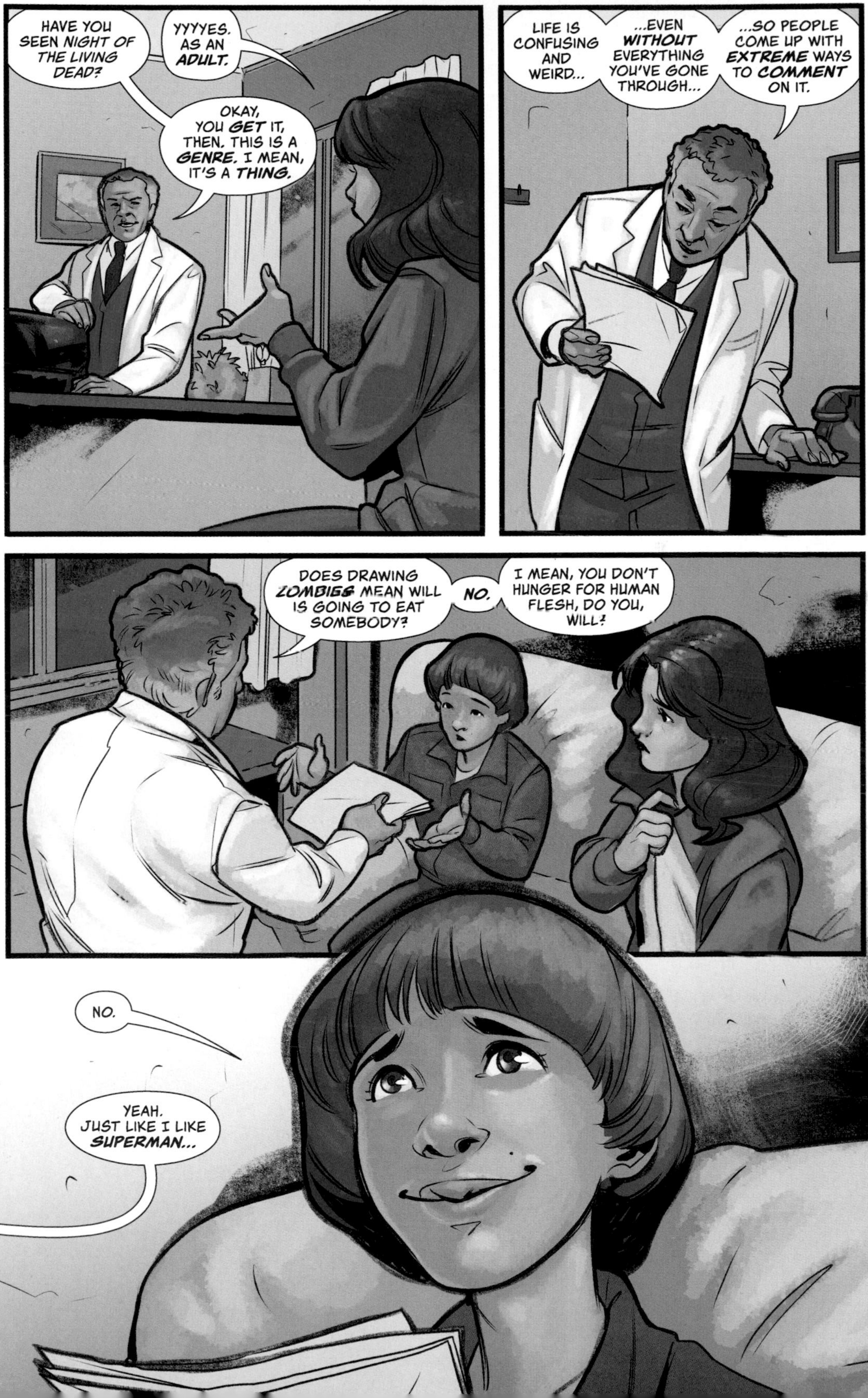
HAVE YOU SEEN NIGHT OF THE LIVING DEAD?
YYYYES. AS AN ADULT.
OKAY, YOU GET IT, THEN. THIS IS A GENRE. I MEAN, IT'S A THING.
LIFE IS CONFUSING AND WEIRD...
...EVEN WITHOUT EVERYTHING YOU'VE GONE THROUGH...
...SO PEOPLE COME UP WITH EXTREME WAYS TO COMMENT ON IT.
DOES DRAWING ZOMBIES MEAN WILL IS GOING TO EAT SOMEBODY?
NO.
I MEAN, YOU DON'T HUNGER FOR HUMAN FLESH, DO YOU, WILL?
NO.
YEAH. JUST LIKE I LIKE SUPERMAN...

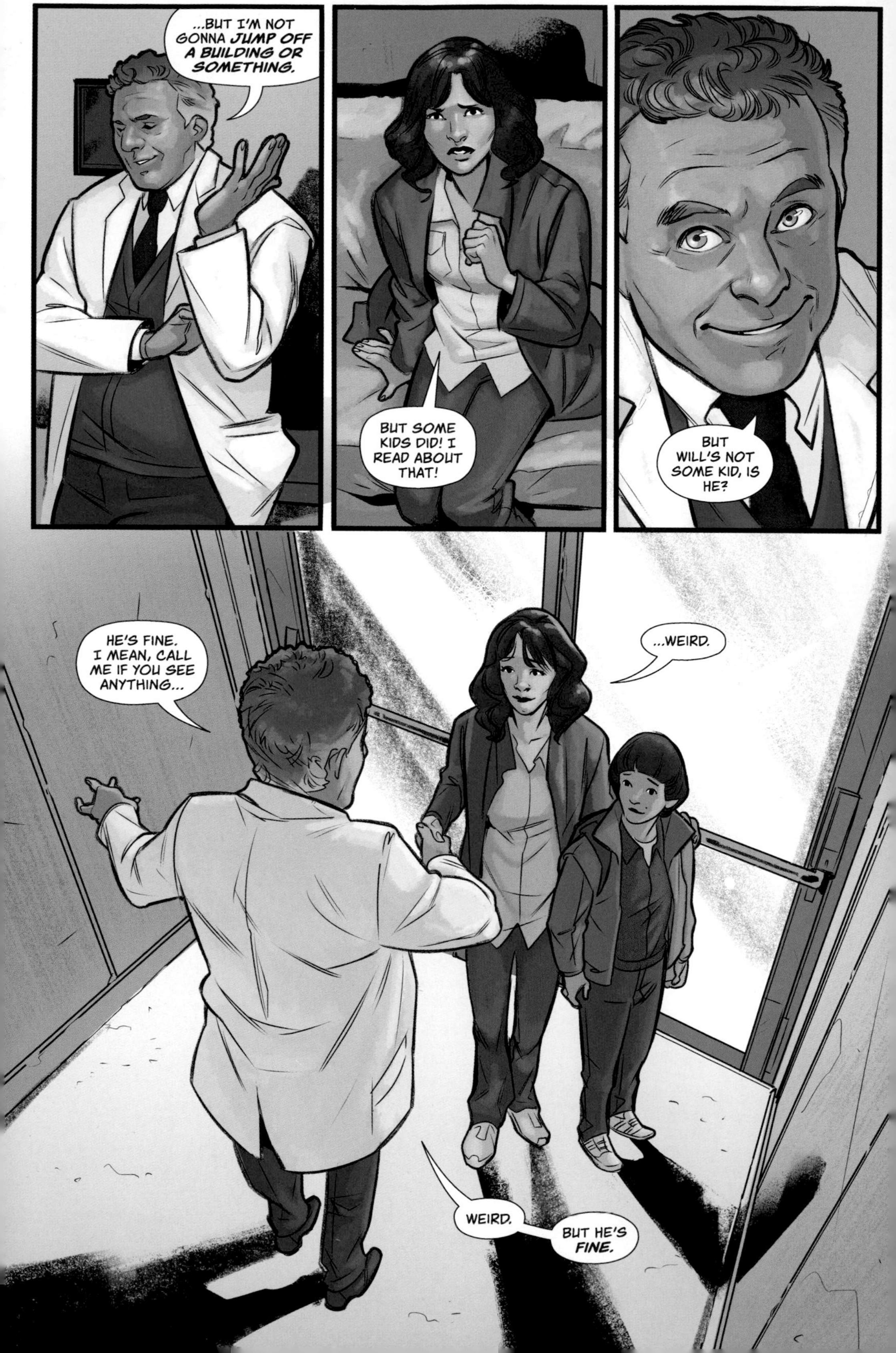

...BUT I'M NOT GONNA *JUMP OFF A BUILDING OR SOMETHING.*
BUT SOME KIDS DID! I READ ABOUT THAT!
BUT WILL'S NOT SOME KID, IS HE?
HE'S FINE. I MEAN, CALL ME IF YOU SEE ANYTHING...
...WEIRD.
WEIRD.
BUT HE'S *FINE.*

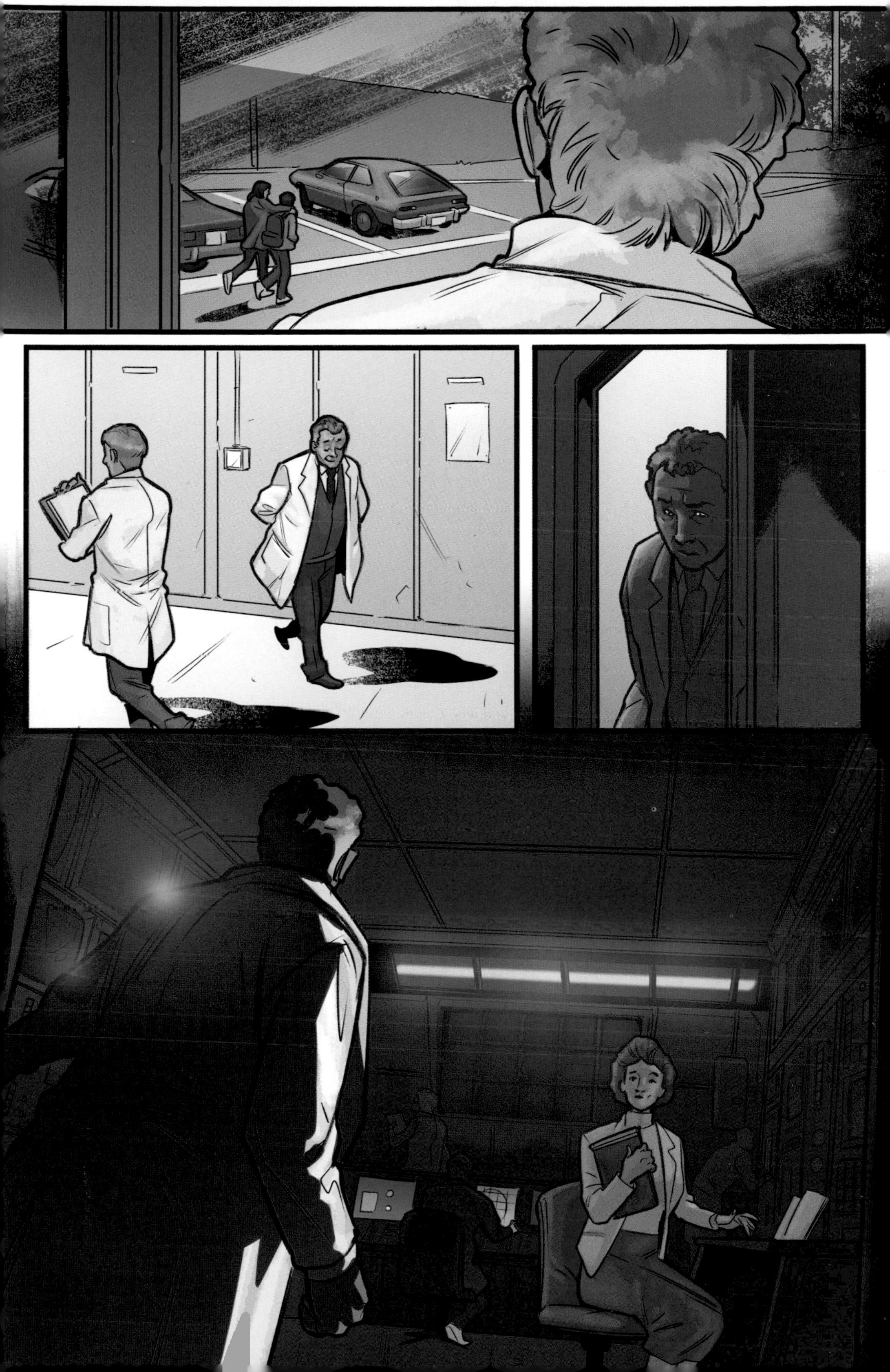

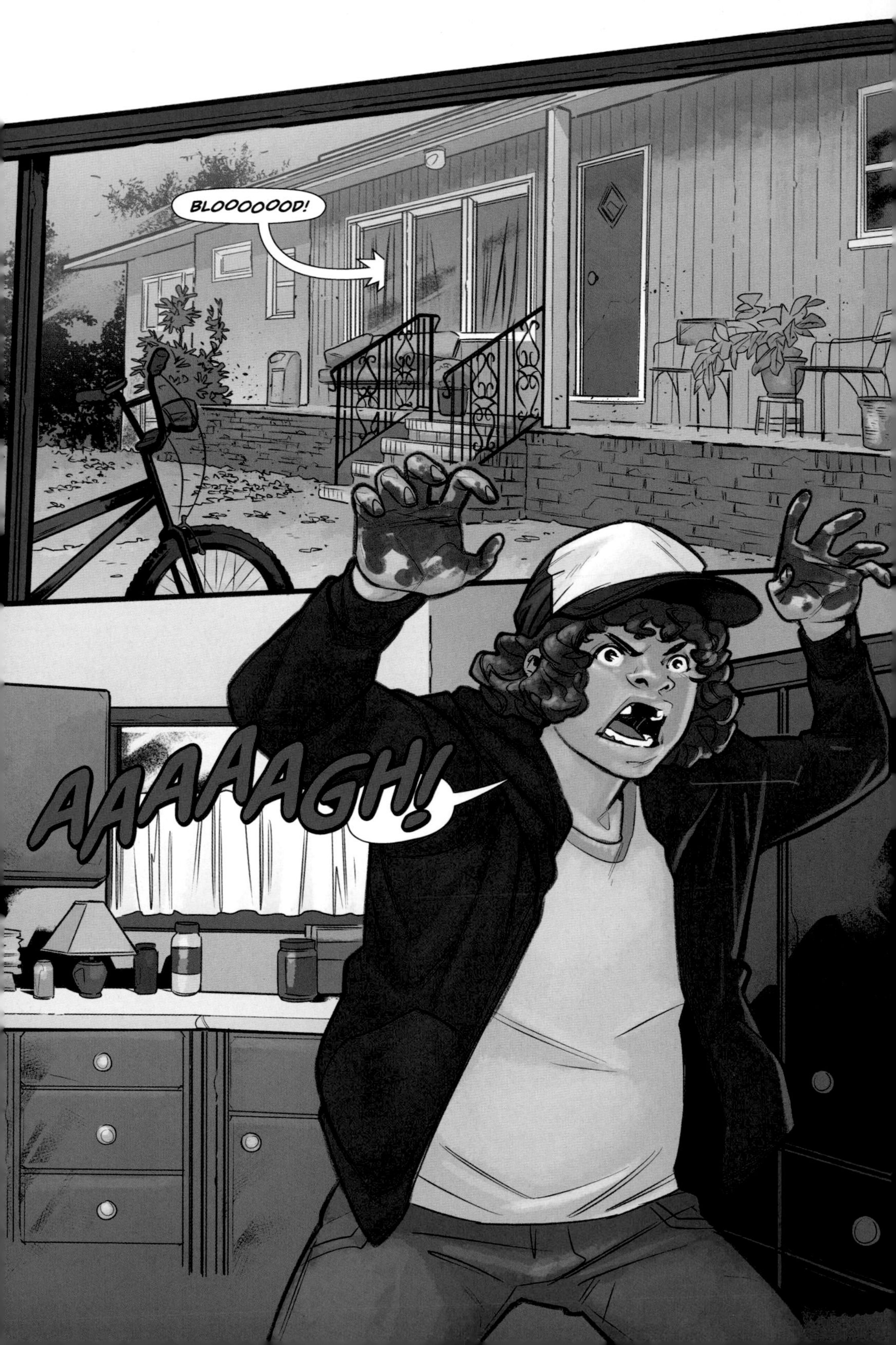
BLOOOOOOD!
AAAAAGH!

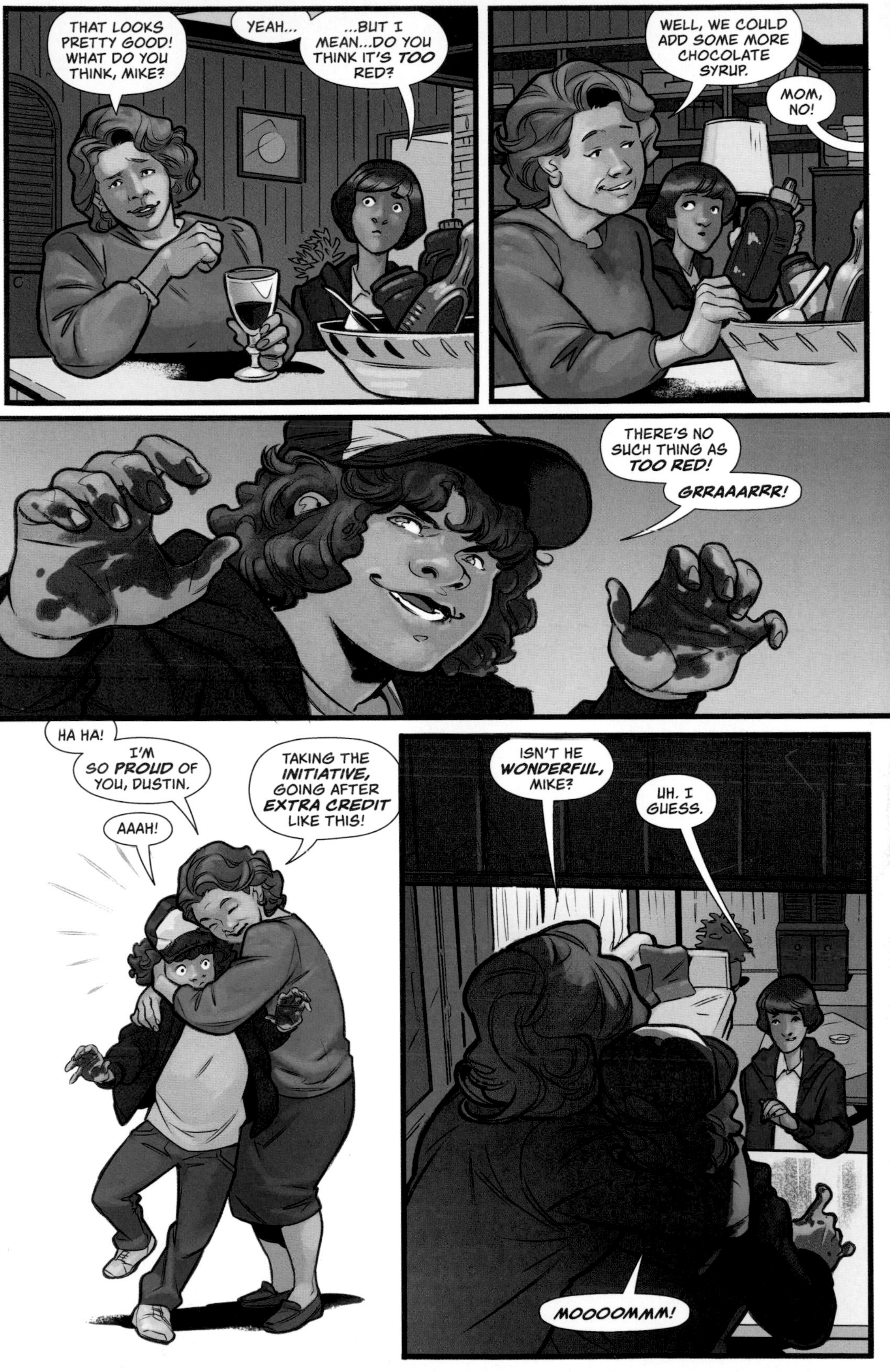

THAT LOOKS PRETTY GOOD! WHAT DO YOU THINK, MIKE?
YEAH...
...BUT I MEAN...DO YOU THINK IT'S TOO RED?
WELL, WE COULD ADD SOME MORE CHOCOLATE SYRUP.
MOM, NO!
THERE'S NO SUCH THING AS TOO RED!
GRRAAARRR!
HA HA!
I'M SO PROUD OF YOU, DUSTIN.
AAAH!
TAKING THE INITIATIVE, GOING AFTER EXTRA CREDIT LIKE THIS!
ISN'T HE WONDERFUL, MIKE?
UH. I GUESS.
MOOOOMMM!

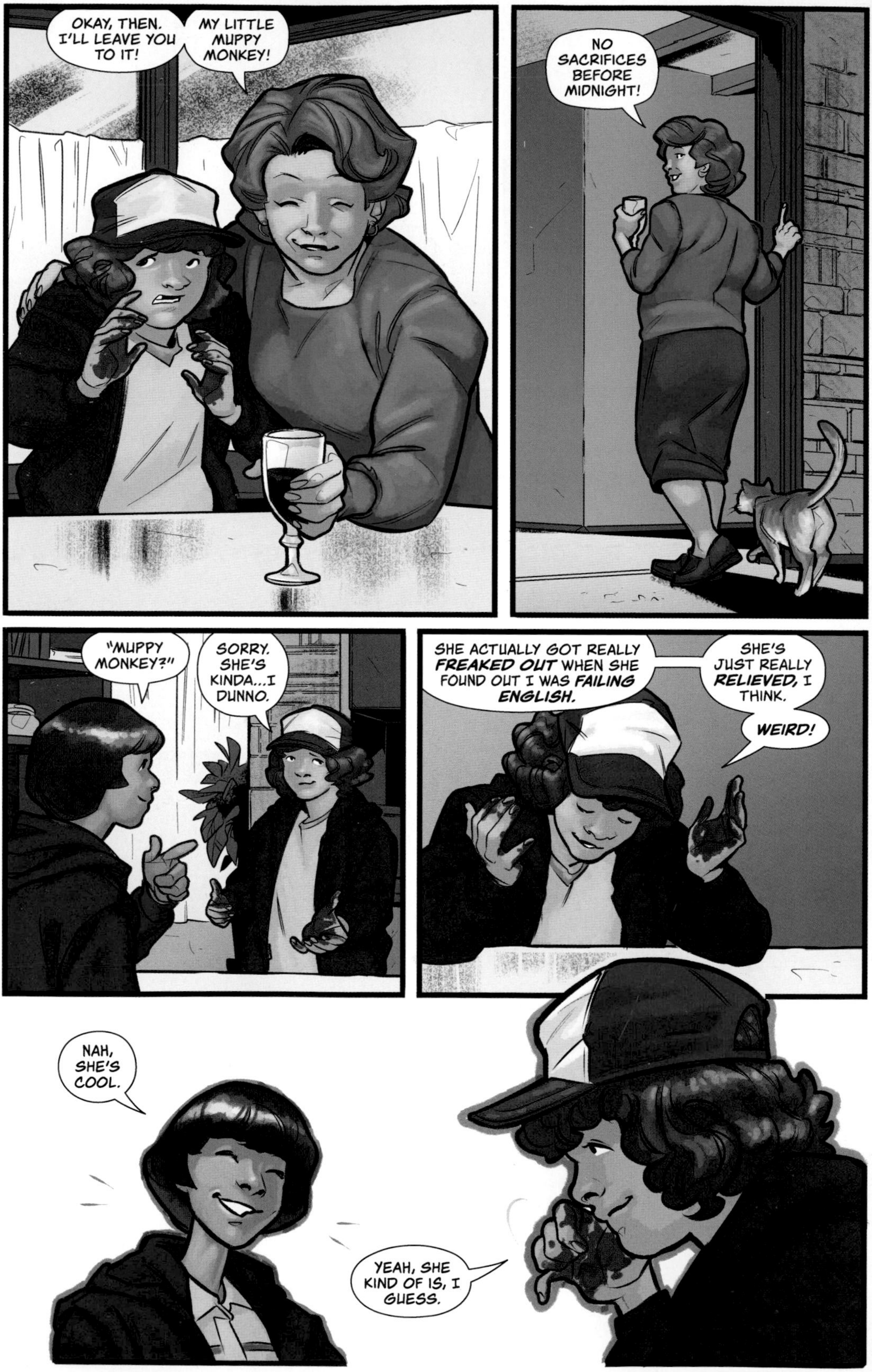
OKAY, THEN. I'LL LEAVE YOU TO IT!
MY LITTLE MUPPY MONKEY!
NO SACRIFICES BEFORE MIDNIGHT!
"MUPPY MONKEY?"
SORRY. SHE'S KINDA...I DUNNO.
SHE ACTUALLY GOT REALLY FREAKED OUT WHEN SHE FOUND OUT I WAS FAILING ENGLISH.
SHE'S JUST REALLY RELIEVED, I THINK.
WEIRD!
NAH, SHE'S COOL.
YEAH, SHE KIND OF IS, I GUESS.

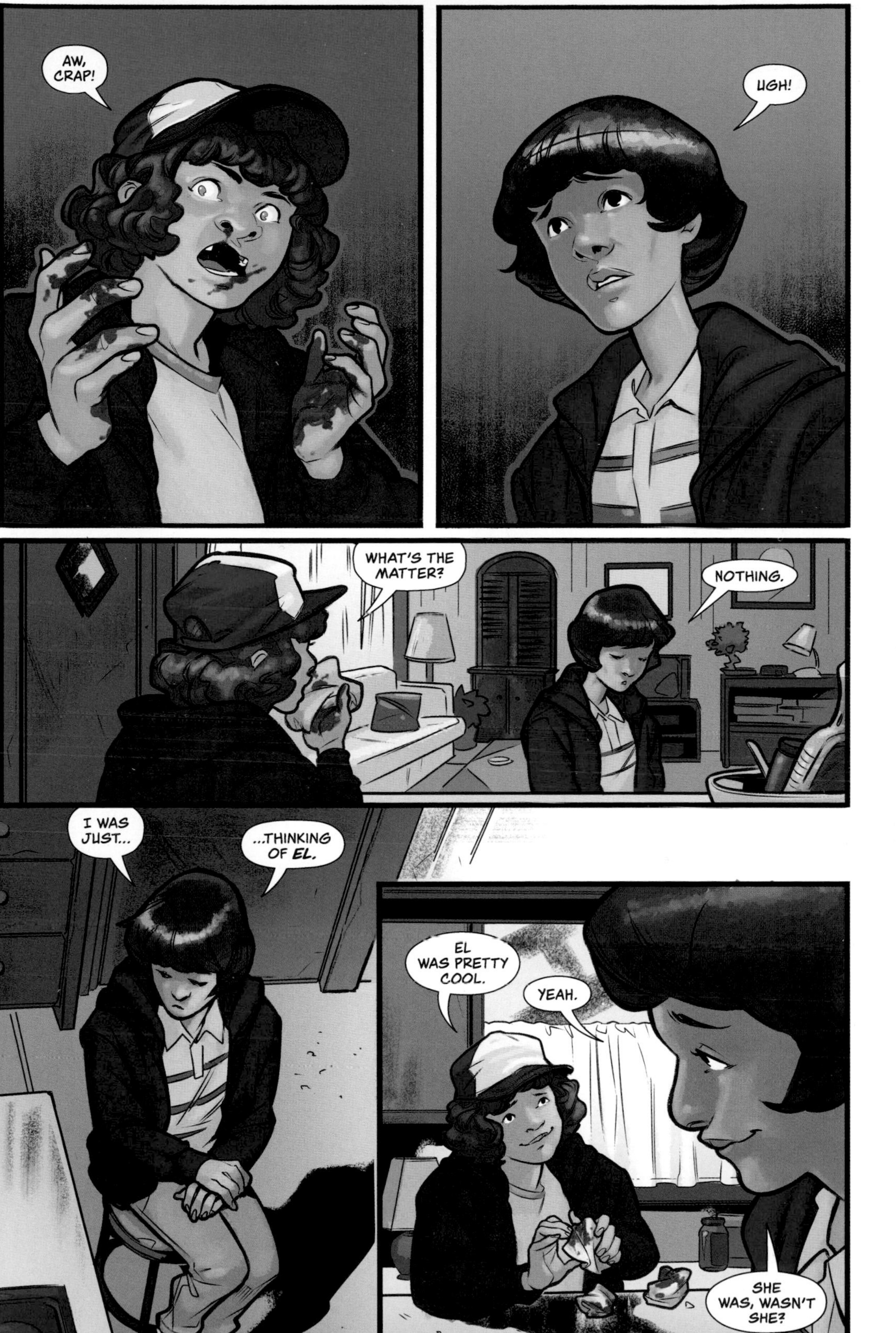
AW, CRAP!
UGH!
WHAT'S THE MATTER?
NOTHING.
I WAS JUST...
...THINKING OF EL.
EL WAS PRETTY COOL.
YEAH.
SHE WAS, WASN'T SHE?

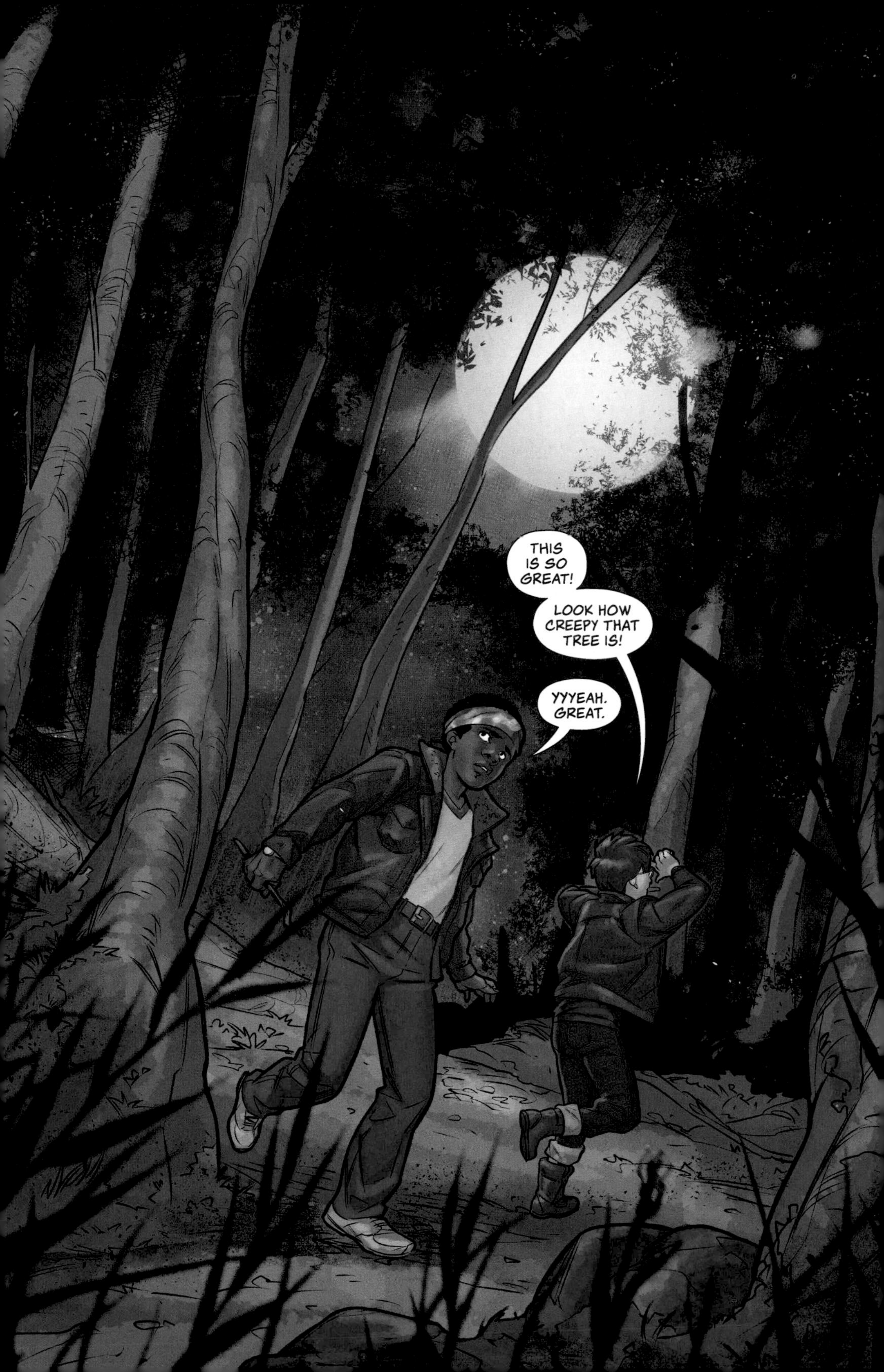
THIS IS SO GREAT!
LOOK HOW CREEPY THAT TREE IS!
YYYEAH. GREAT.

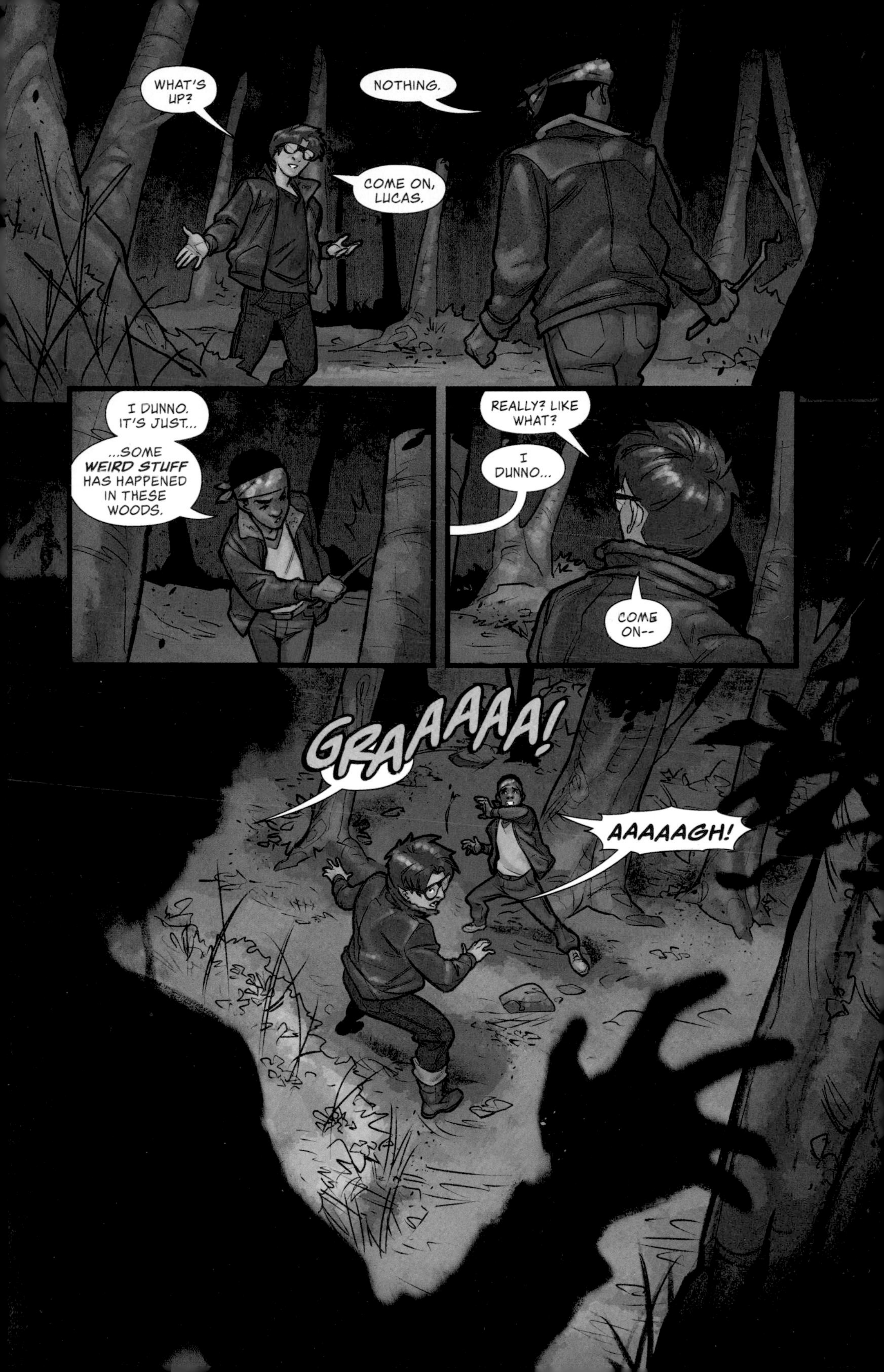
WHAT'S UP?
NOTHING.
COME ON, LUCAS.
I DUNNO. IT'S JUST...
...SOME WEIRD STUFF HAS HAPPENED IN THESE WOODS.
REALLY? LIKE WHAT?
I DUNNO...
COME ON--
GRAAAAAA!
AAAAAGH!

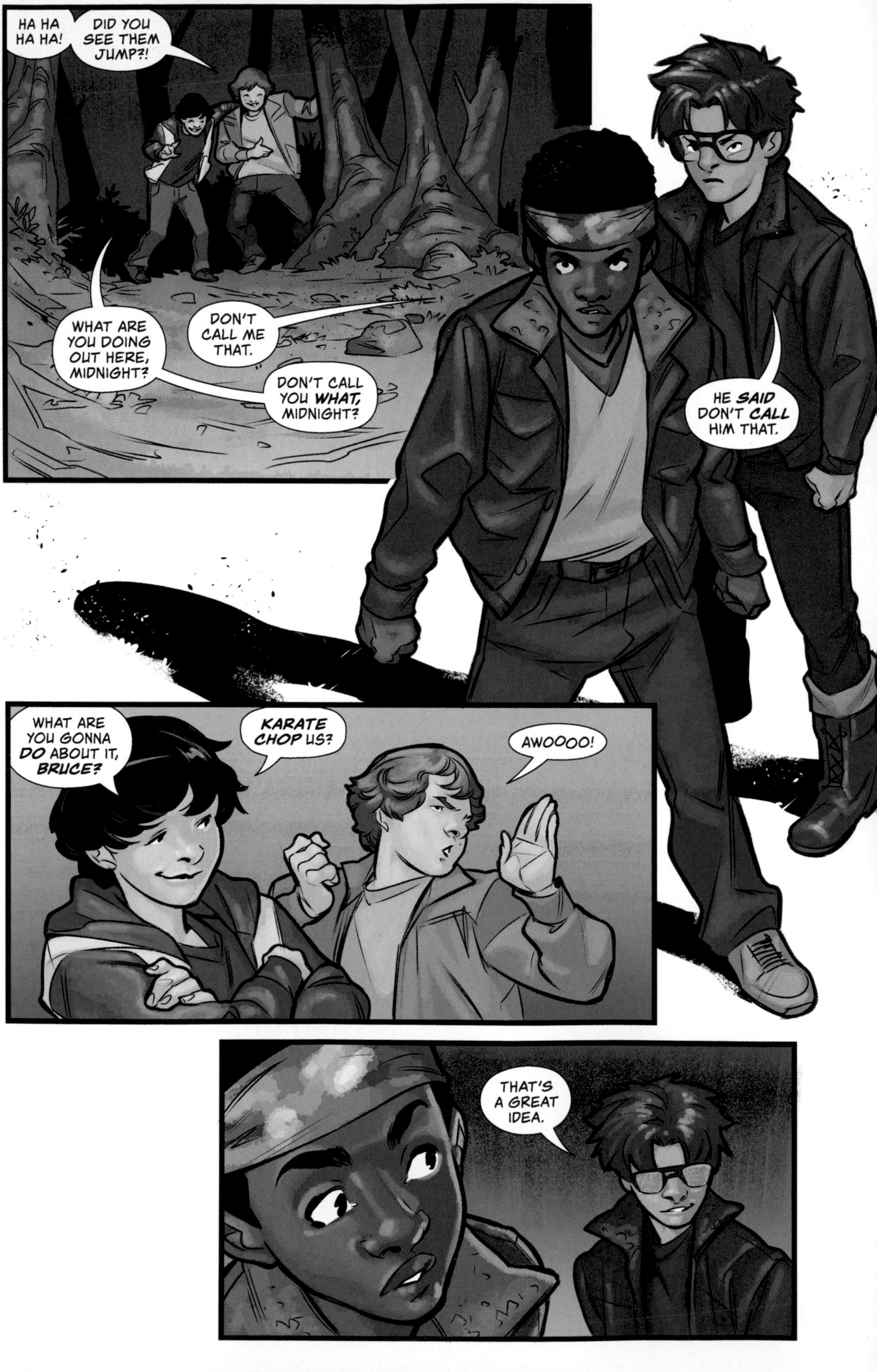
HA HA HA HA!
DID YOU SEE THEM JUMP?!
WHAT ARE YOU DOING OUT HERE, MIDNIGHT?
DON'T CALL ME THAT.
DON'T CALL YOU WHAT, MIDNIGHT?
HE SAID DON'T CALL HIM THAT.
WHAT ARE YOU GONNA DO ABOUT IT, BRUCE?
KARATE CHOP US?
AWOOOO!
THAT'S A GREAT IDEA.

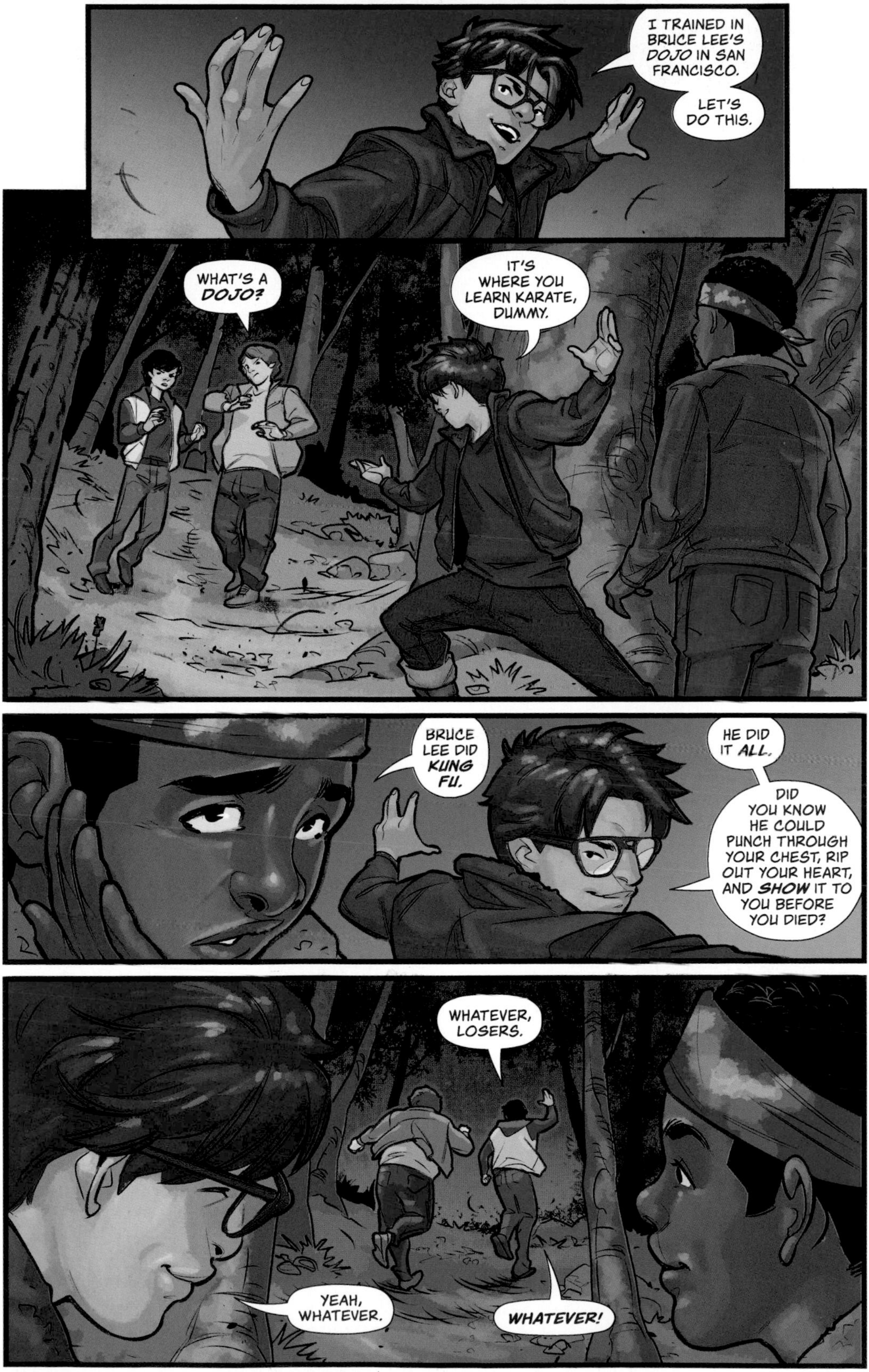
I TRAINED IN BRUCE LEE'S DOJO IN SAN FRANCISCO.
LET'S DO THIS.
WHAT'S A DOJO?
IT'S WHERE YOU LEARN KARATE, DUMMY.
BRUCE LEE DID KUNG FU.
HE DID IT ALL.
DID YOU KNOW HE COULD PUNCH THROUGH YOUR CHEST, RIP OUT YOUR HEART, AND SHOW IT TO YOU BEFORE YOU DIED?
WHATEVER, LOSERS.
YEAH, WHATEVER.
WHATEVER!

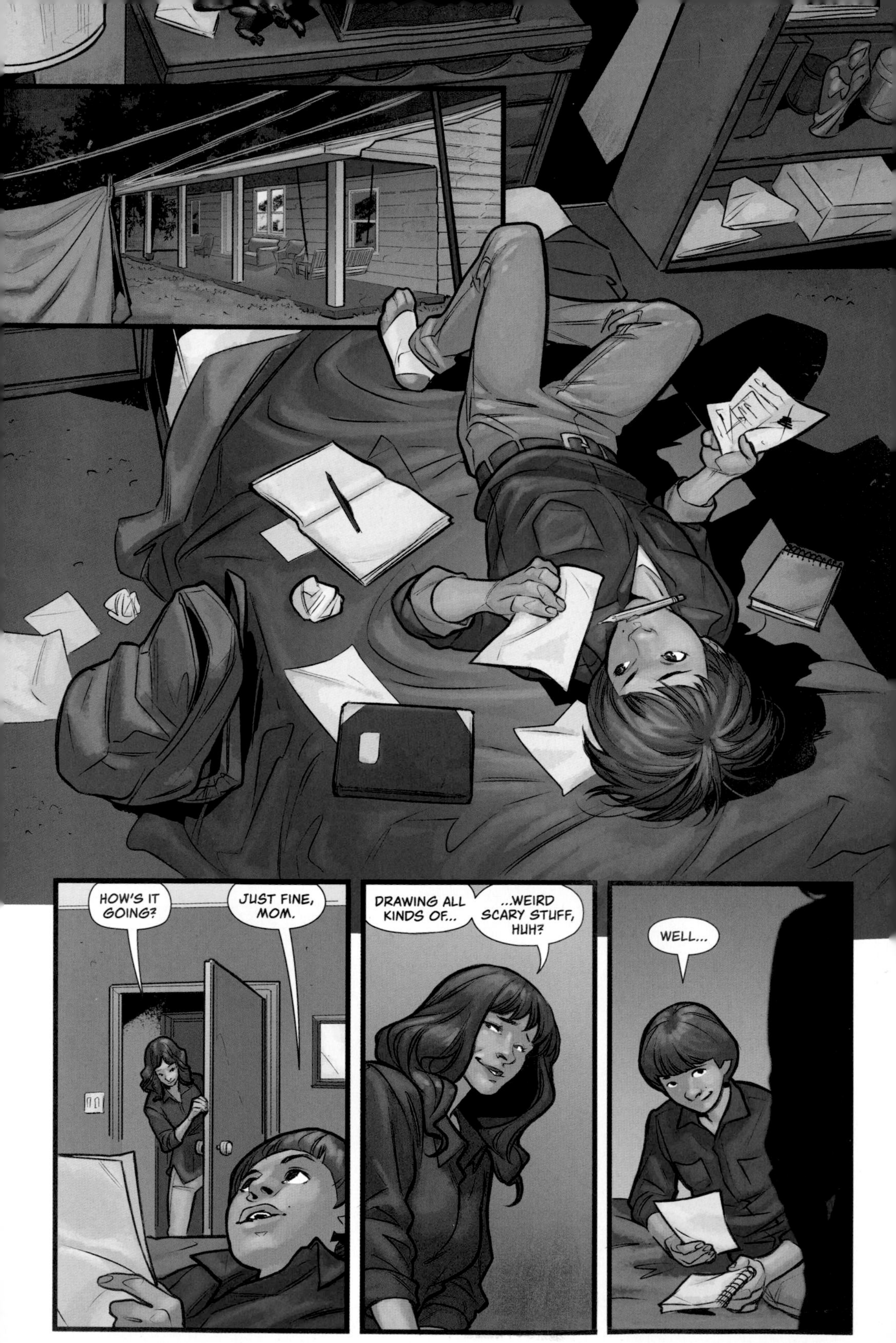
HOW'S IT GOING?
JUST FINE, MOM.
DRAWING ALL KINDS OF...
...WEIRD SCARY STUFF, HUH?
WELL...

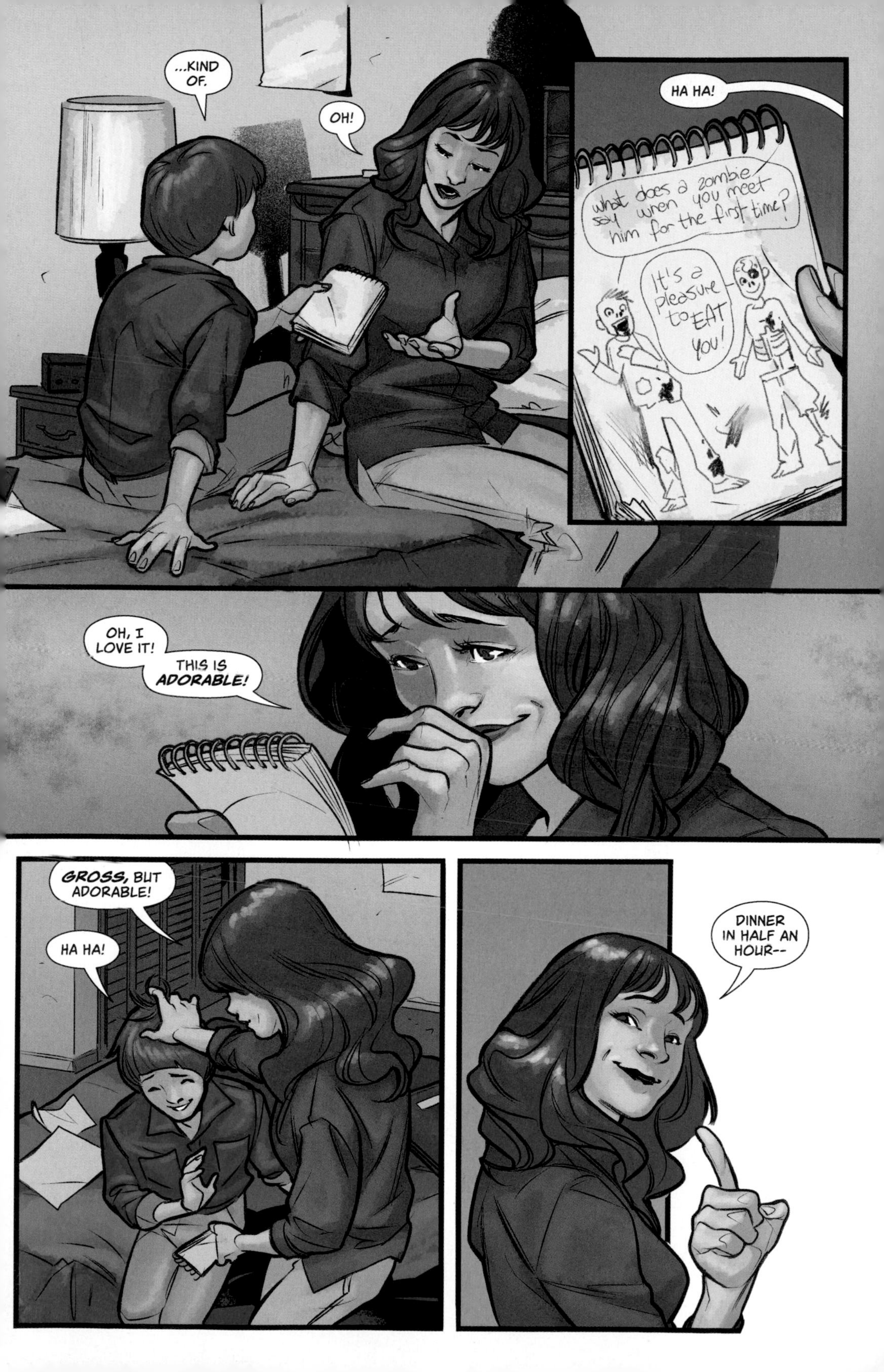
...KIND OF.
OH!
HA HA!
what does a zombie say when you meet him for the first time?
It's a pleasure to EAT you!
OH, I LOVE IT!
THIS IS ADORABLE!
GROSS, BUT ADORABLE!
HA HA!
DINNER IN HALF AN HOUR--

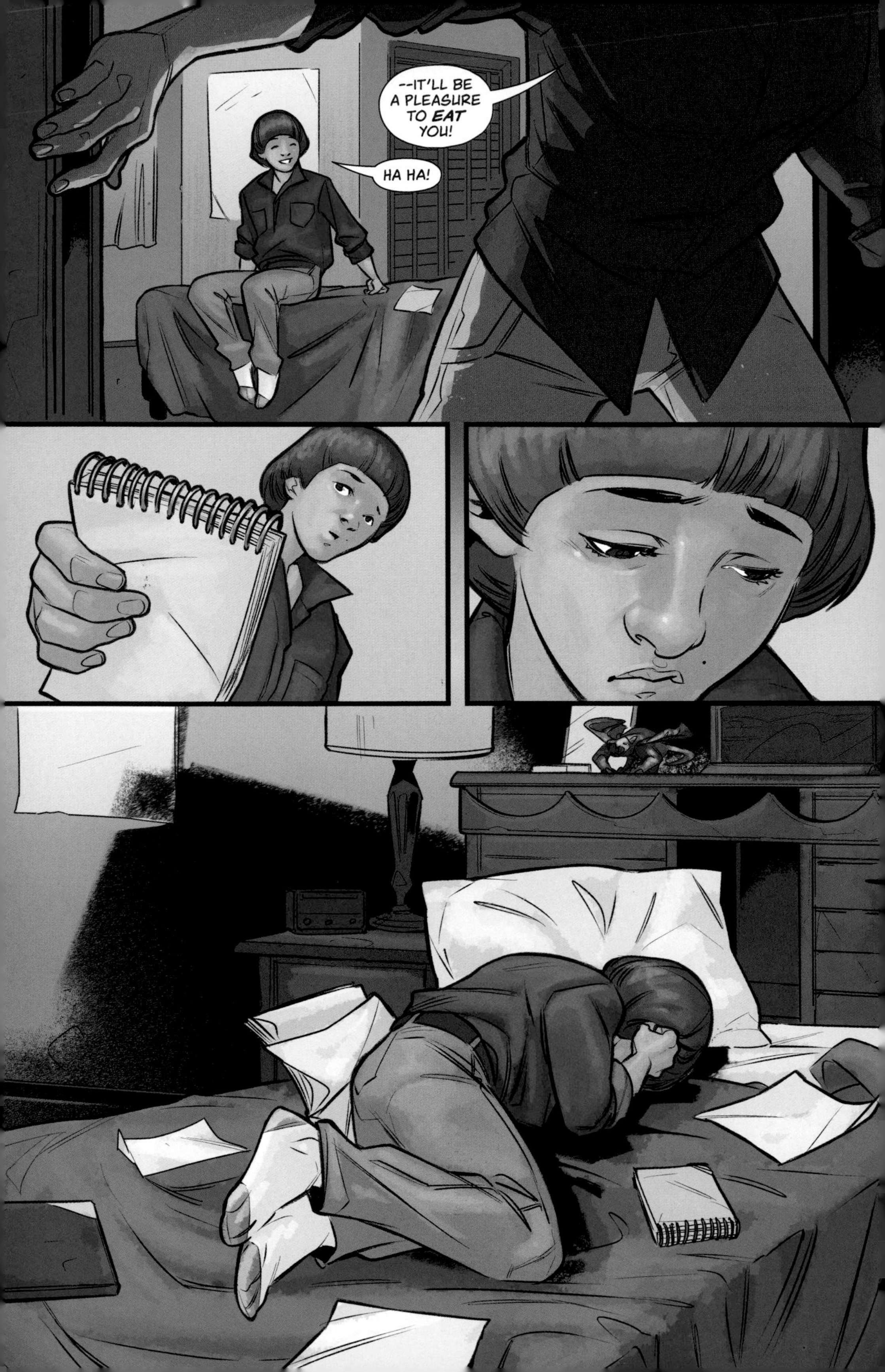
--IT'LL BE A PLEASURE TO EAT YOU!
HA HA!

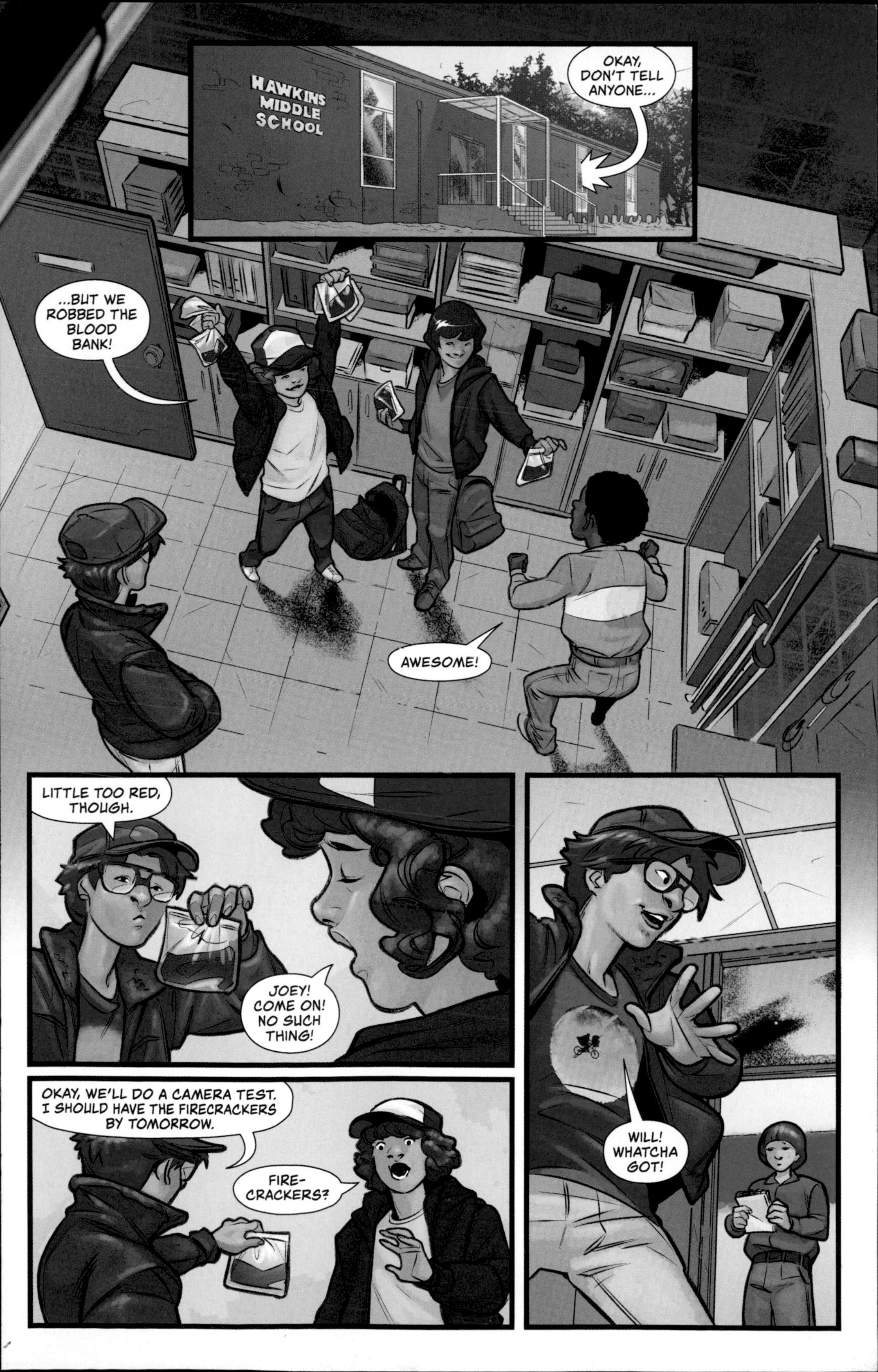
HAWKINS MIDDLE SCHOOL
OKAY, DON'T TELL ANYONE...
...BUT WE ROBBED THE BLOOD BANK!
AWESOME!
LITTLE TOO RED, THOUGH.
JOEY! COME ON! NO SUCH THING!
OKAY, WE'LL DO A CAMERA TEST. I SHOULD HAVE THE FIRECRACKERS BY TOMORROW.
FIRE-CRACKERS?
WILL! WHATCHA GOT!

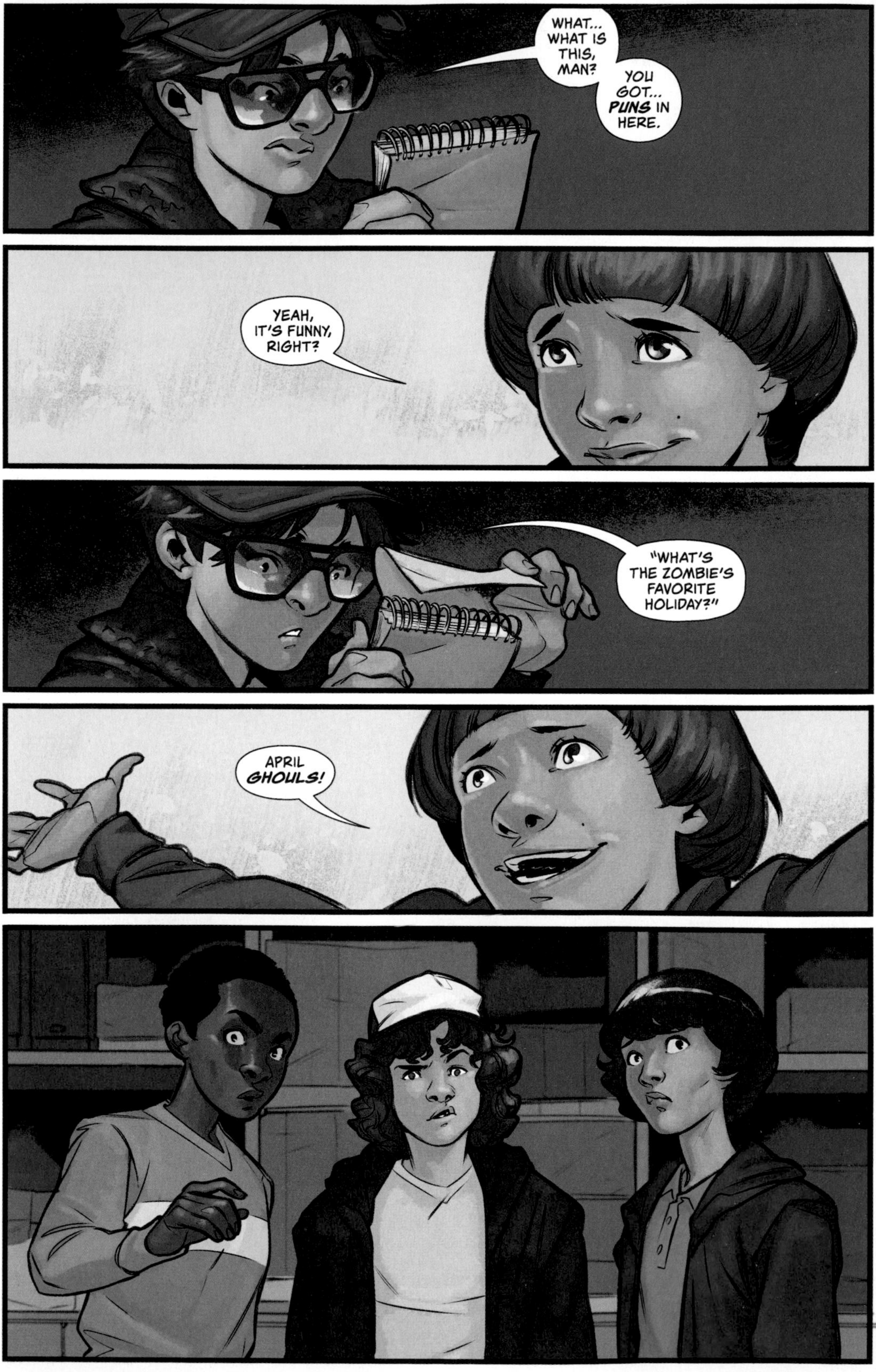
WHAT... WHAT IS THIS, MAN?
YOU GOT... PUNS IN HERE.
YEAH, IT'S FUNNY, RIGHT?
"WHAT'S THE ZOMBIE'S FAVORITE HOLIDAY?"
APRIL GHOULS!

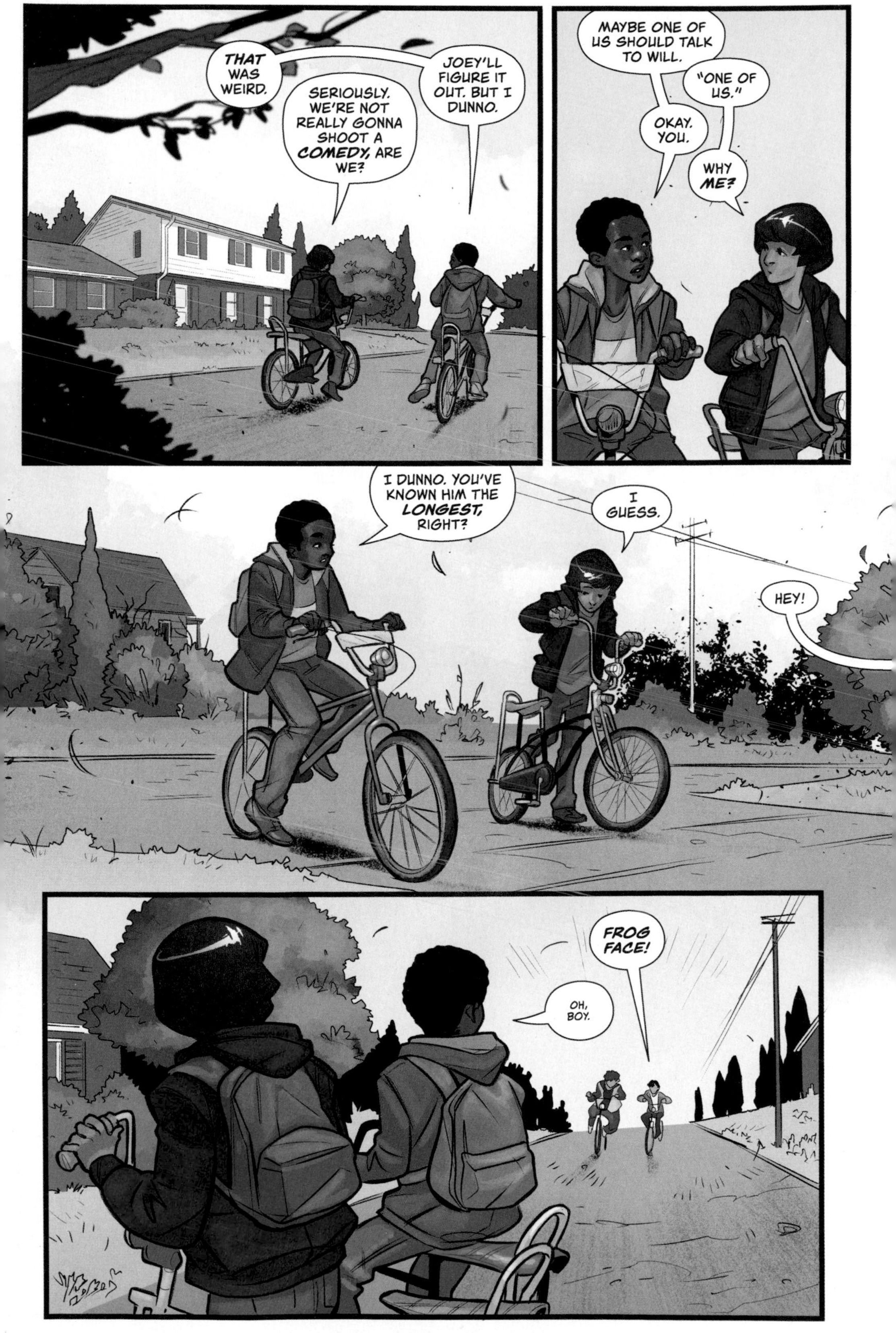
THAT WAS WEIRD.
SERIOUSLY. WE'RE NOT REALLY GONNA SHOOT A COMEDY, ARE WE?
JOEY'LL FIGURE IT OUT. BUT I DUNNO.
MAYBE ONE OF US SHOULD TALK TO WILL.
"ONE OF US."
OKAY. YOU.
WHY ME?
I DUNNO. YOU'VE KNOWN HIM THE LONGEST, RIGHT?
I GUESS.
HEY!
FROG FACE!
OH, BOY.

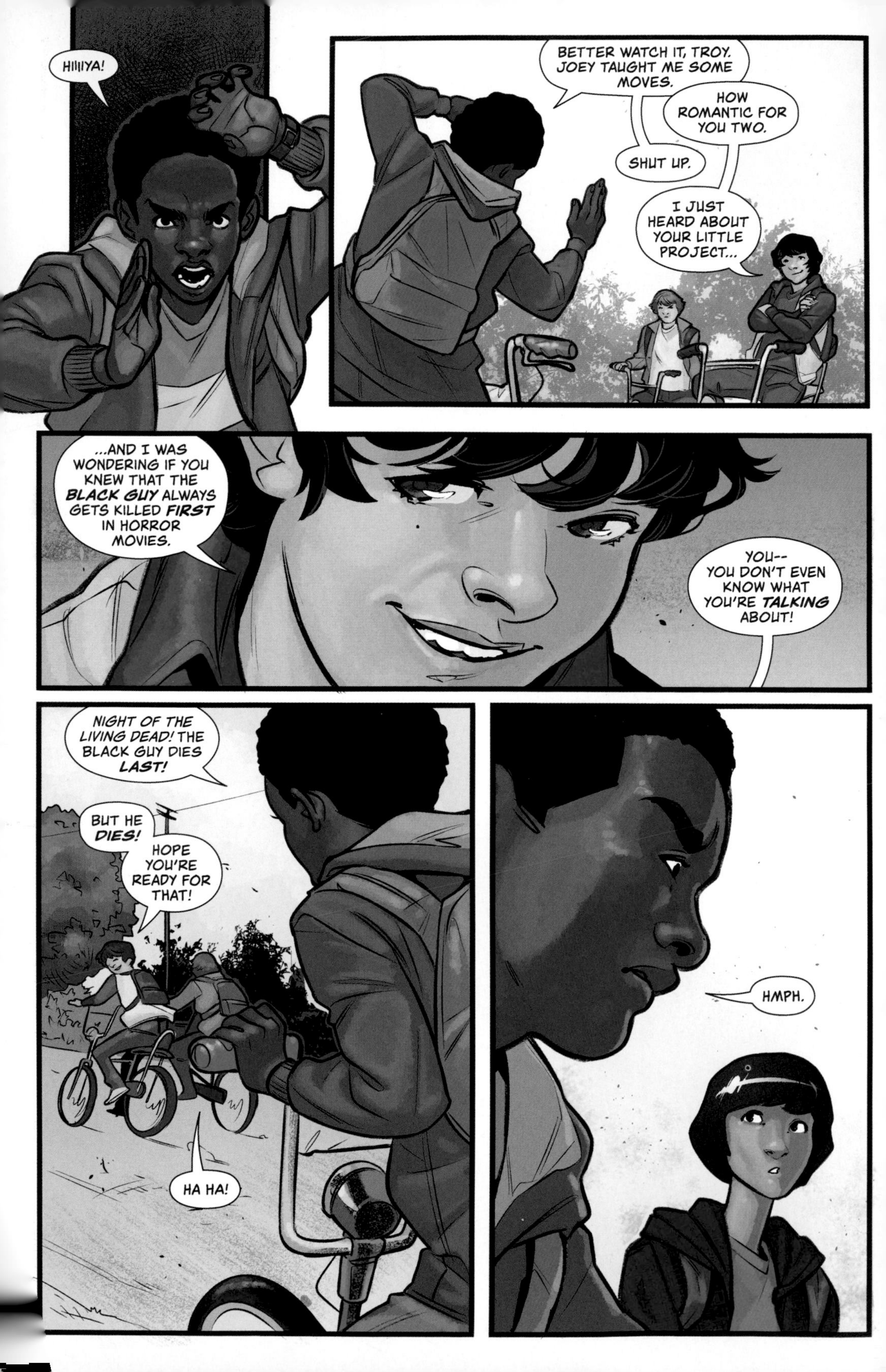
HIIIIYA!
BETTER WATCH IT, TROY. JOEY TAUGHT ME SOME MOVES.
HOW ROMANTIC FOR YOU TWO.
SHUT UP.
I JUST HEARD ABOUT YOUR LITTLE PROJECT...
...AND I WAS WONDERING IF YOU KNEW THAT THE BLACK GUY ALWAYS GETS KILLED FIRST IN HORROR MOVIES.
YOU-- YOU DON'T EVEN KNOW WHAT YOU'RE TALKING ABOUT!
NIGHT OF THE LIVING DEAD! THE BLACK GUY DIES LAST!
BUT HE DIES!
HOPE YOU'RE READY FOR THAT!
HA HA!
HMPH.

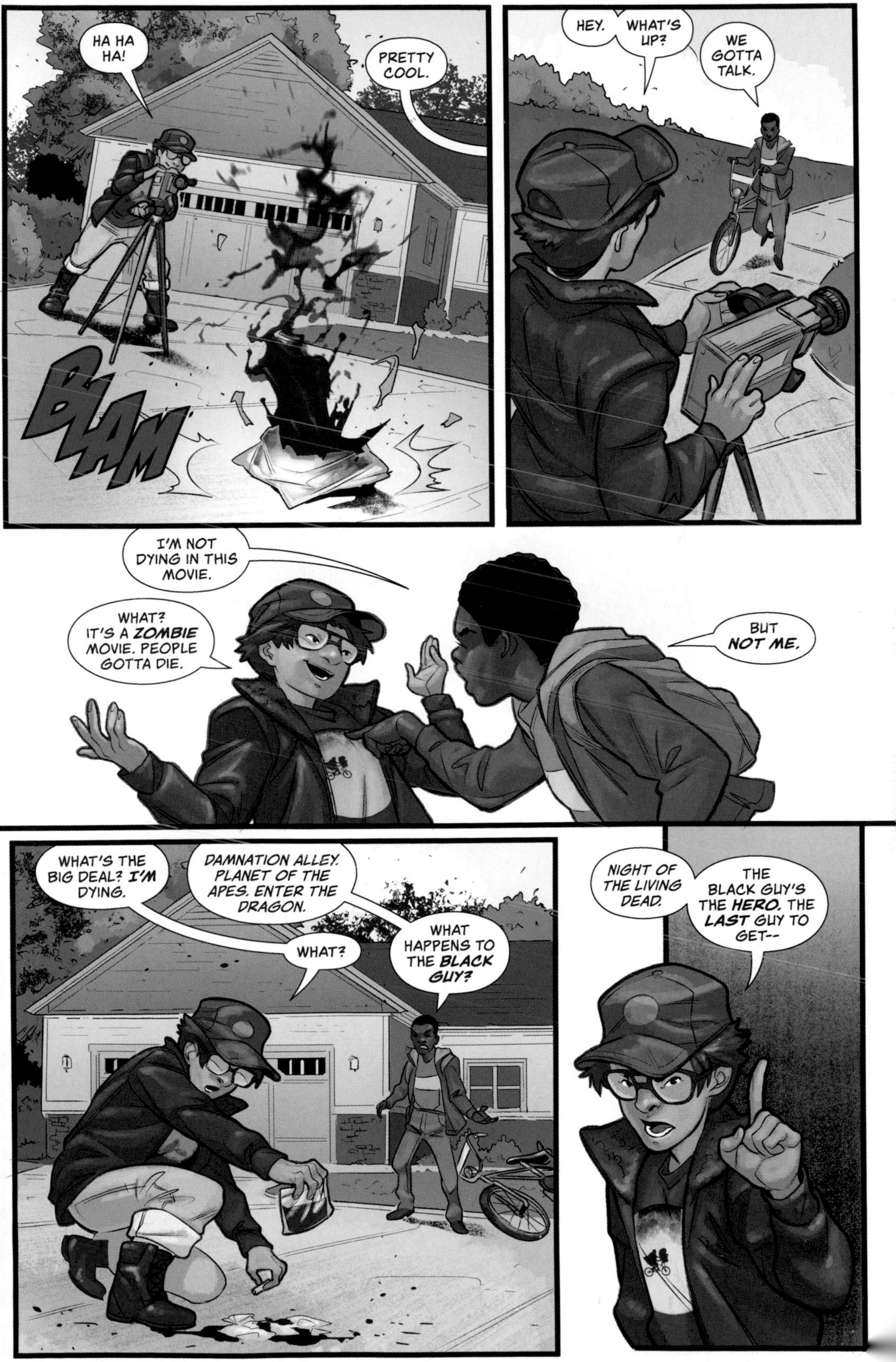
HA HA HA!
PRETTY COOL.
BLAM
HEY.
WHAT'S UP?
WE GOTTA TALK.
I'M NOT DYING IN THIS MOVIE.
WHAT? IT'S A ZOMBIE MOVIE. PEOPLE GOTTA DIE.
BUT NOT ME.
WHAT'S THE BIG DEAL? I'M DYING.
DAMNATION ALLEY. PLANET OF THE APES. ENTER THE DRAGON.
WHAT?
WHAT HAPPENS TO THE BLACK GUY?
NIGHT OF THE LIVING DEAD.
THE BLACK GUY'S THE HERO. THE LAST GUY TO GET--

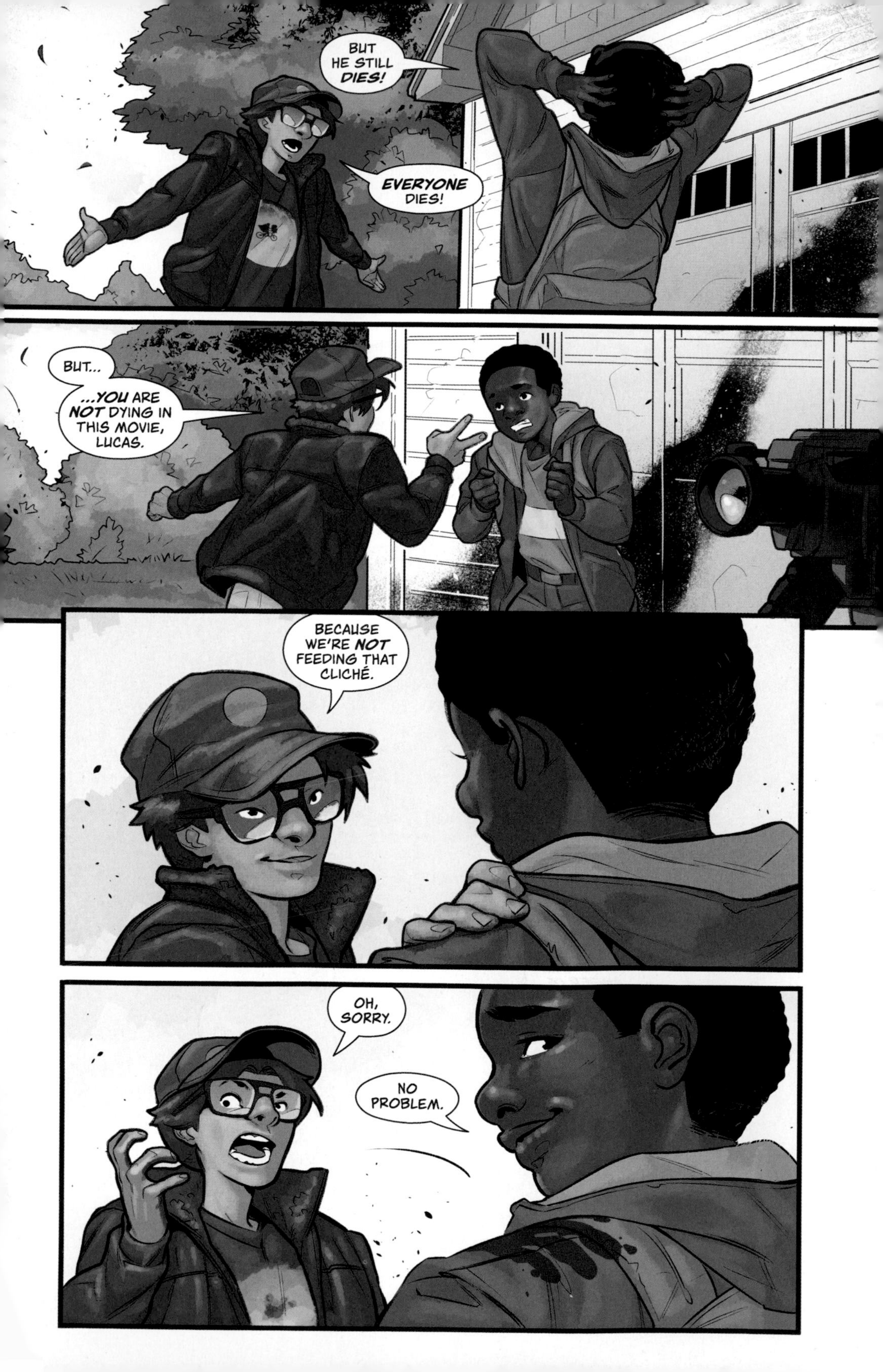
BUT HE STILL DIES!
EVERYONE DIES!
BUT...
...YOU ARE NOT DYING IN THIS MOVIE, LUCAS.
BECAUSE WE'RE NOT FEEDING THAT CLICHÉ.
OH, SORRY.
NO PROBLEM.

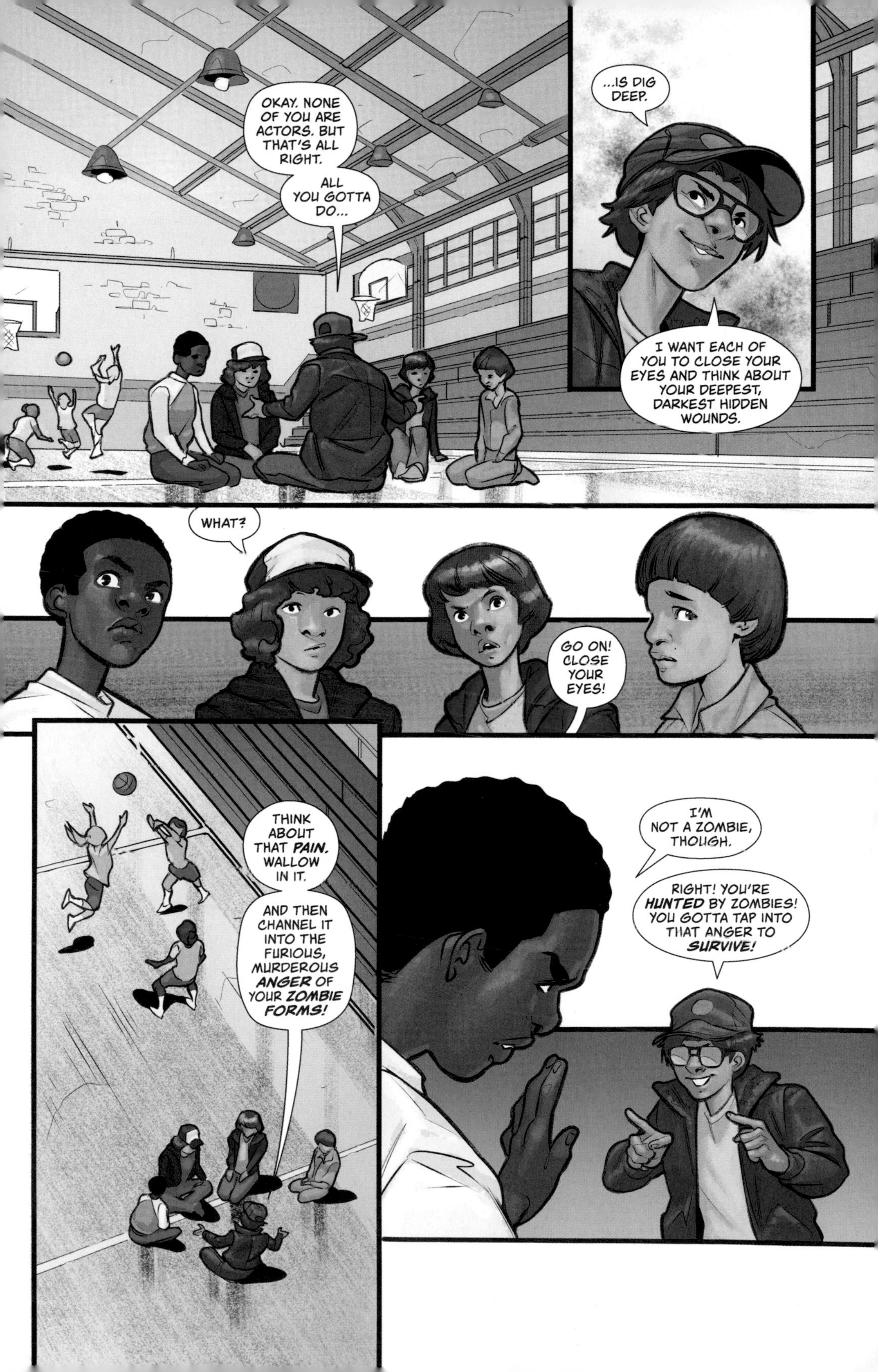
OKAY. NONE OF YOU ARE ACTORS. BUT THAT'S ALL RIGHT.
ALL YOU GOTTA DO...
...IS DIG DEEP.
I WANT EACH OF YOU TO CLOSE YOUR EYES AND THINK ABOUT YOUR DEEPEST, DARKEST HIDDEN WOUNDS.
WHAT?
GO ON! CLOSE YOUR EYES!
THINK ABOUT THAT PAIN. WALLOW IN IT.
AND THEN CHANNEL IT INTO THE FURIOUS, MURDEROUS ANGER OF YOUR ZOMBIE FORMS!
I'M NOT A ZOMBIE, THOUGH.
RIGHT! YOU'RE HUNTED BY ZOMBIES! YOU GOTTA TAP INTO THAT ANGER TO SURVIVE!

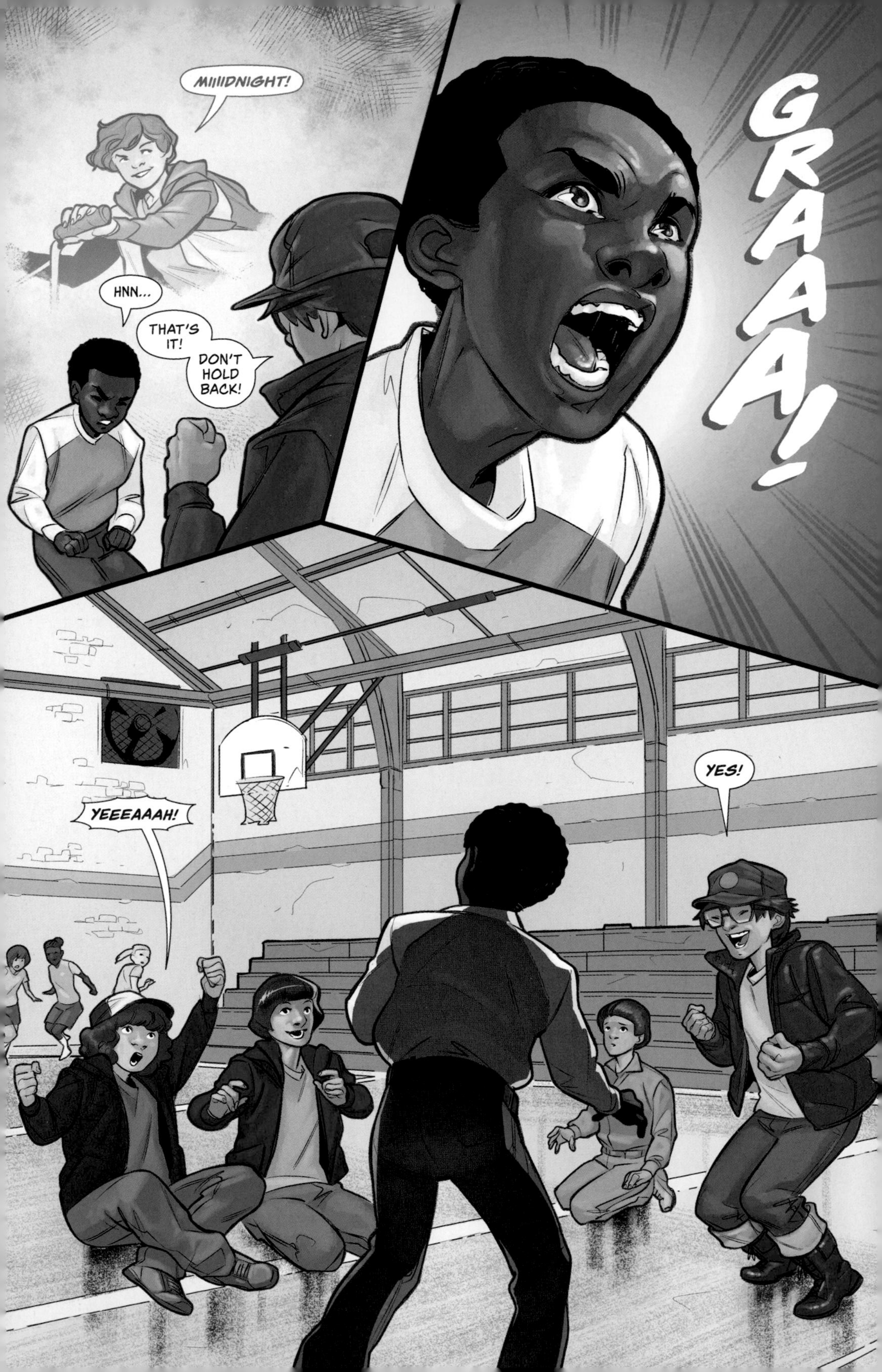

MIIIIDNIGHT!
HNN...
THAT'S IT!
DON'T HOLD BACK!
GRAAA!
YEEEAAAH!
YES!

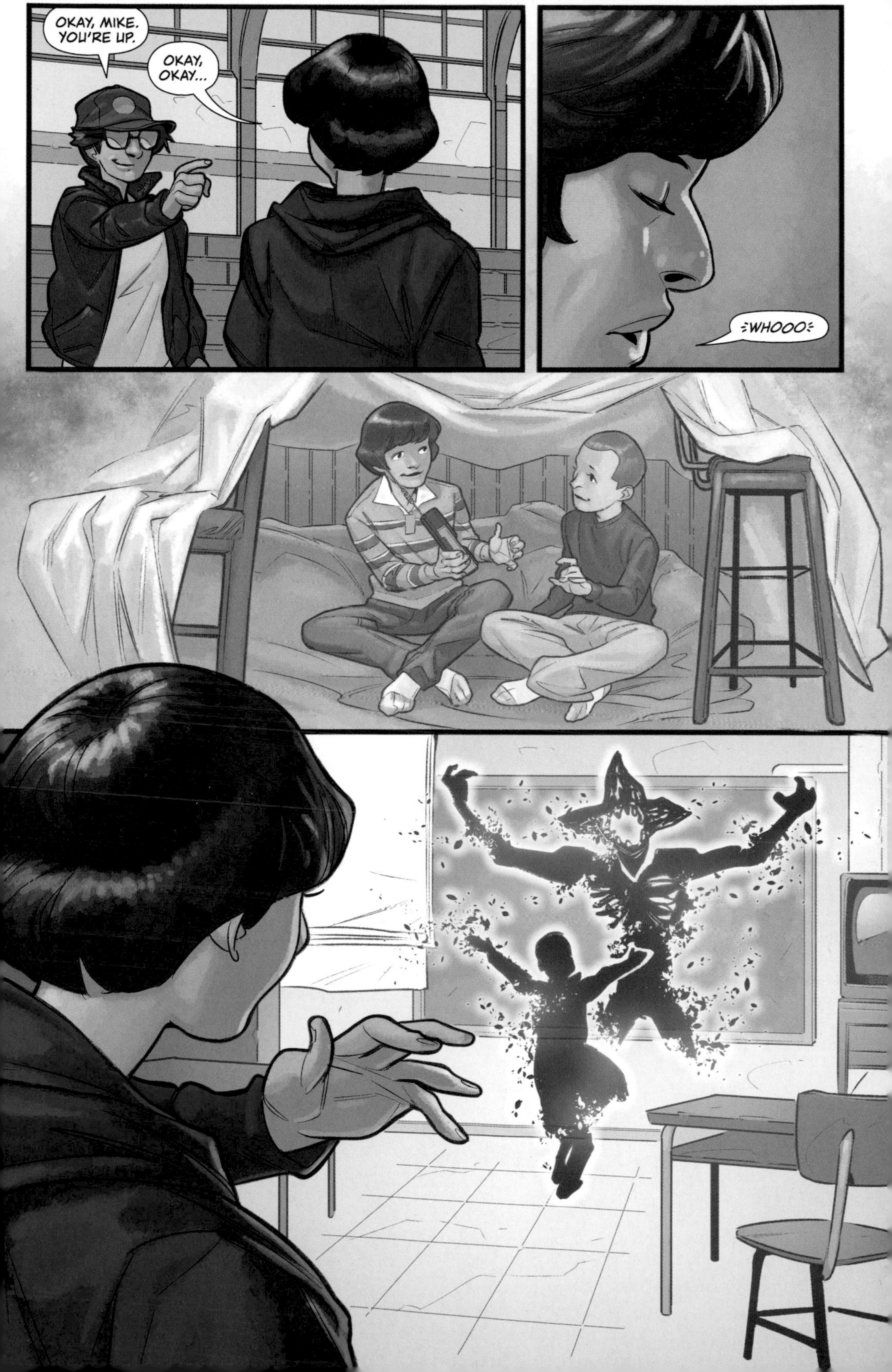
OKAY, MIKE. YOU'RE UP.
OKAY, OKAY...
WHOOO

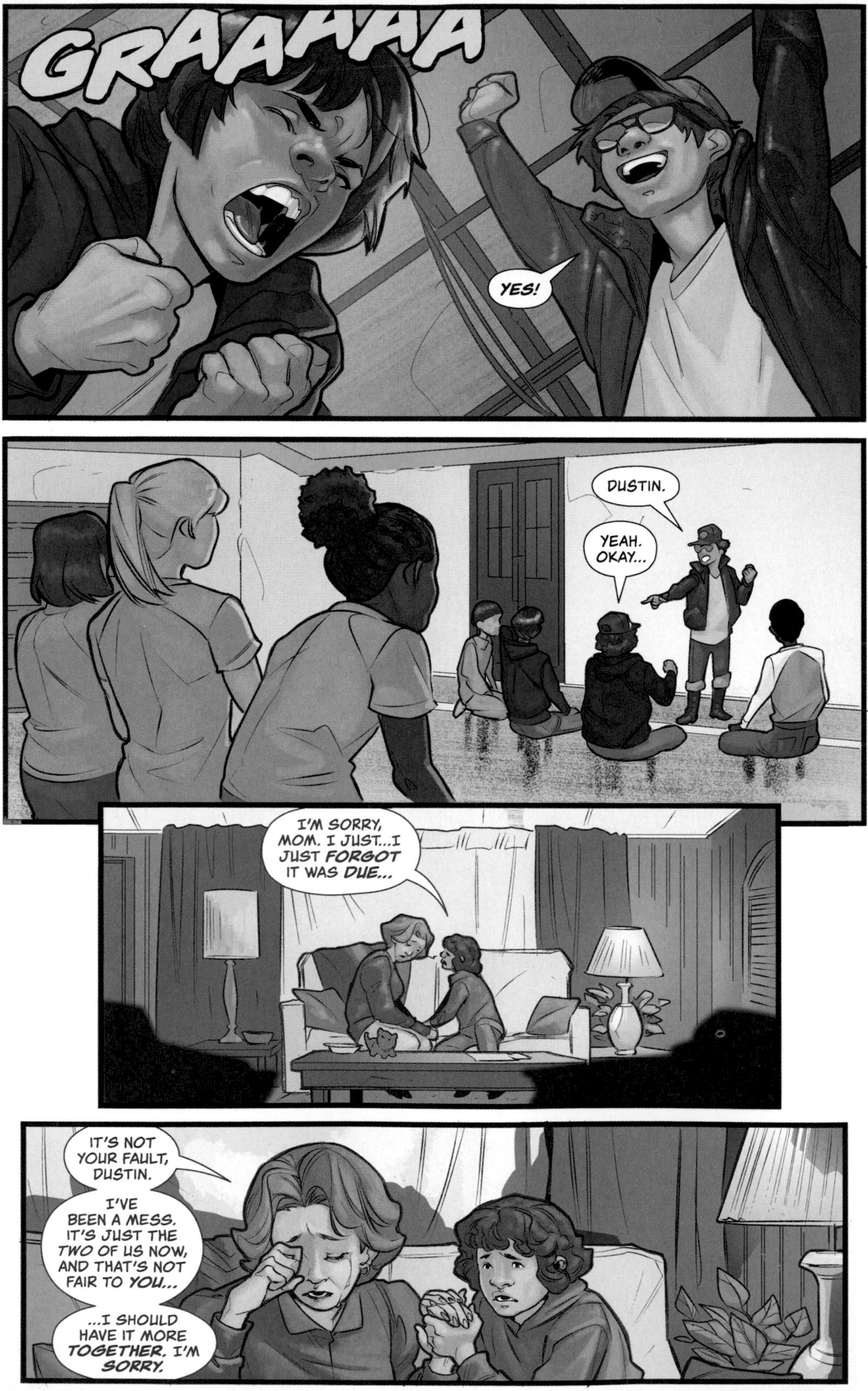
GRAAAAA
YES!
DUSTIN.
YEAH. OKAY...
I'M SORRY, MOM. I JUST...I JUST FORGOT IT WAS DUE...
IT'S NOT YOUR FAULT, DUSTIN.
I'VE BEEN A MESS. IT'S JUST THE TWO OF US NOW, AND THAT'S NOT FAIR TO YOU...
...I SHOULD HAVE IT MORE TOGETHER. I'M SORRY.

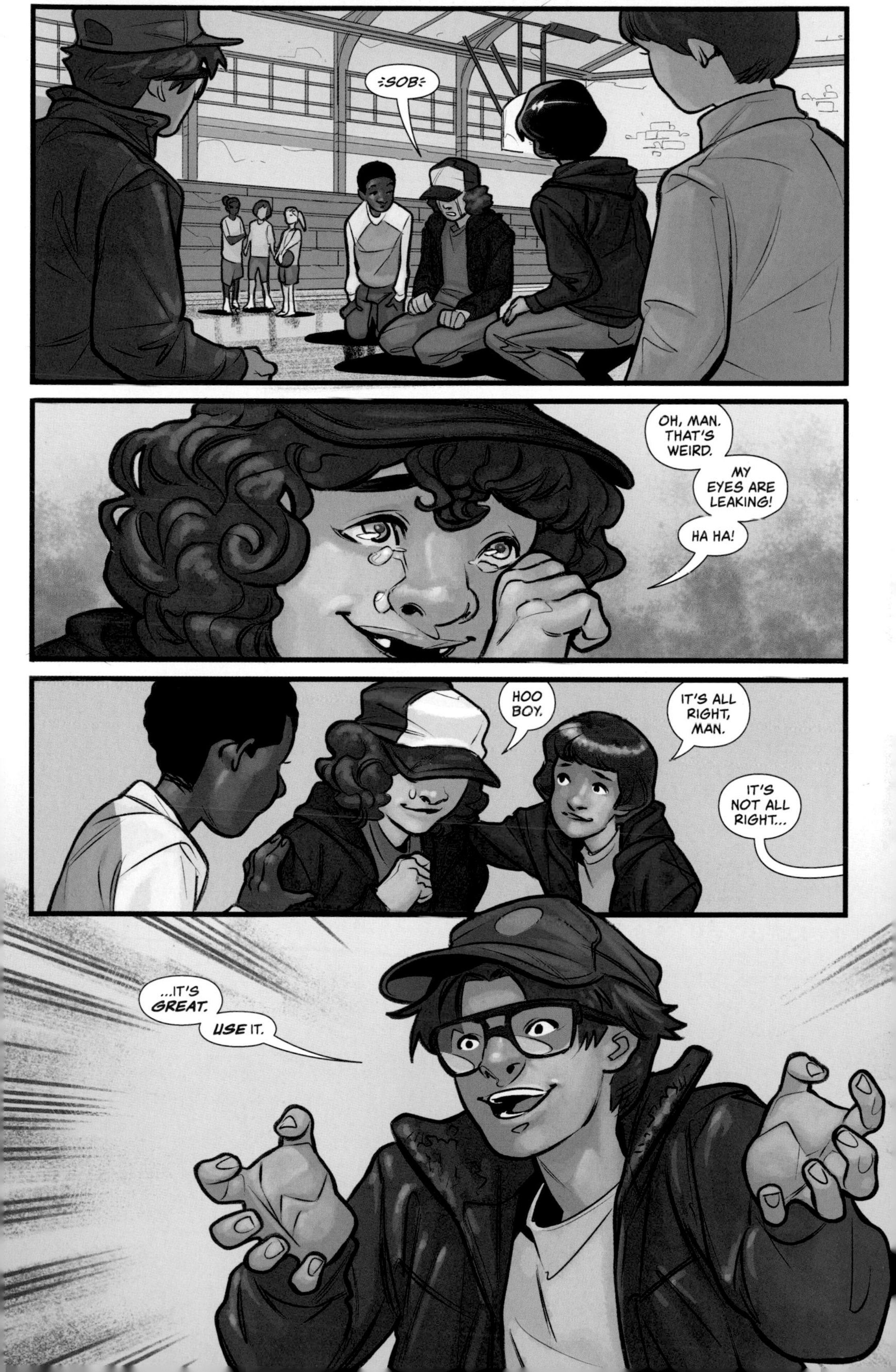

SOB
OH, MAN. THAT'S WEIRD.
MY EYES ARE LEAKING!
HA HA!
HOO BOY.
IT'S ALL RIGHT, MAN.
IT'S NOT ALL RIGHT...
...IT'S GREAT.
USE IT.

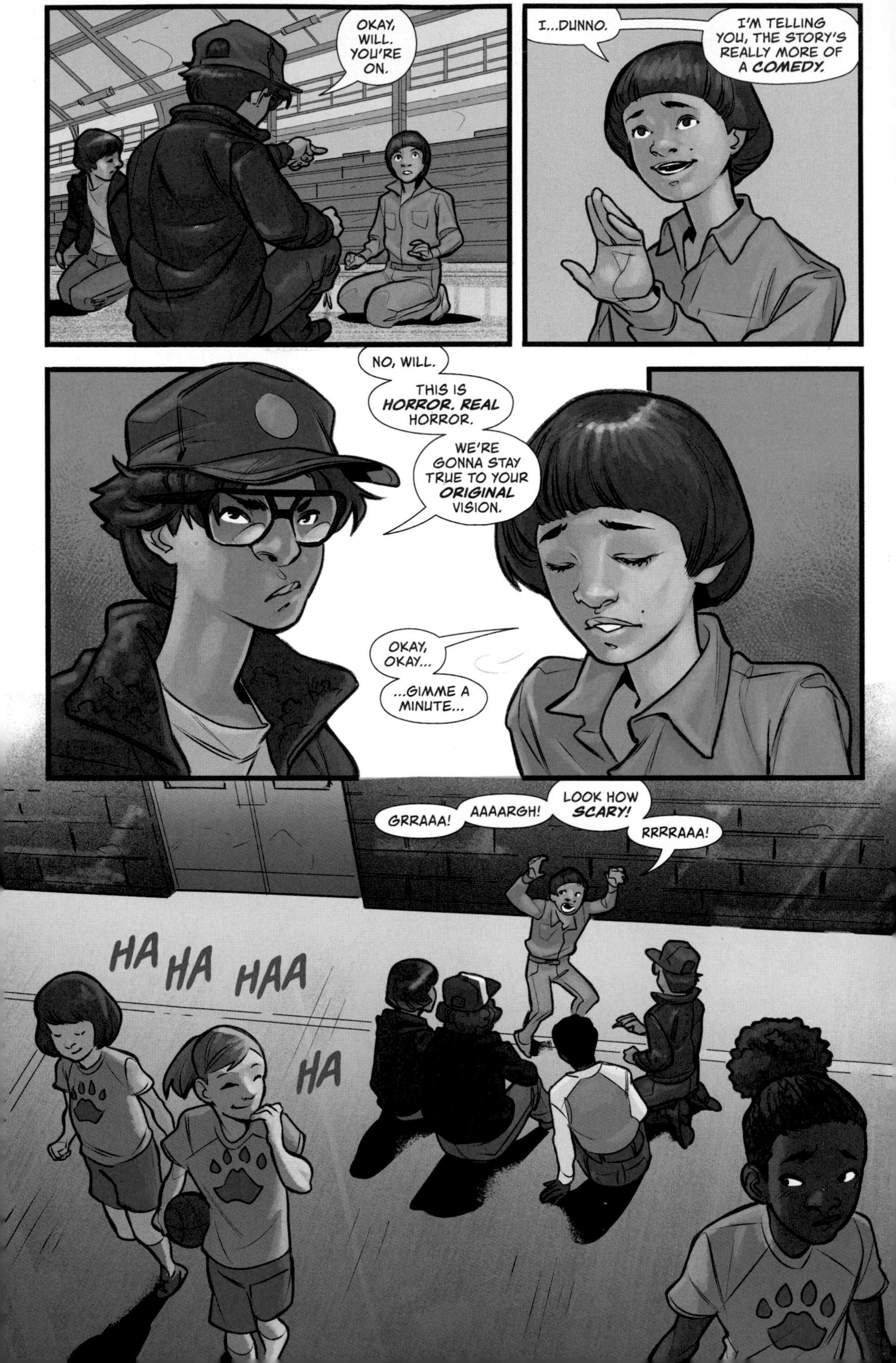
OKAY, WILL. YOU'RE ON.
I...DUNNO.
I'M TELLING YOU, THE STORY'S REALLY MORE OF A **COMEDY.**
NO, WILL.
THIS IS **HORROR. REAL** HORROR.
WE'RE GONNA STAY TRUE TO YOUR **ORIGINAL** VISION.
OKAY, OKAY...
...GIMME A MINUTE...
GRRAAA!
AAAARGH!
LOOK HOW **SCARY!**
RRRRAAA!
HA HA HAA
HA

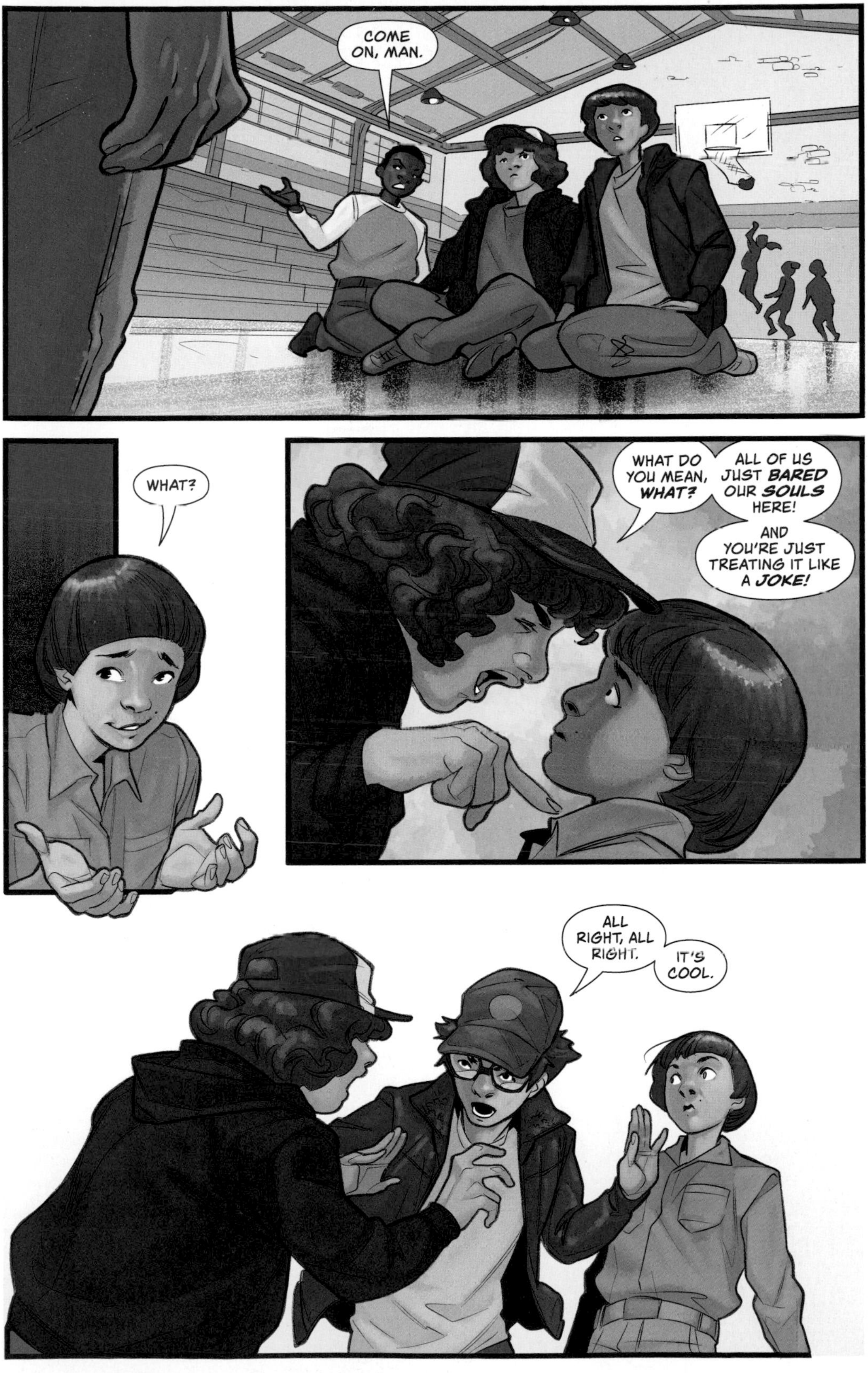
COME ON, MAN.
WHAT?
WHAT DO YOU MEAN, *WHAT?*
ALL OF US JUST *BARED* OUR *SOULS* HERE!
AND YOU'RE JUST TREATING IT LIKE A *JOKE!*
ALL RIGHT, ALL RIGHT.
IT'S COOL.

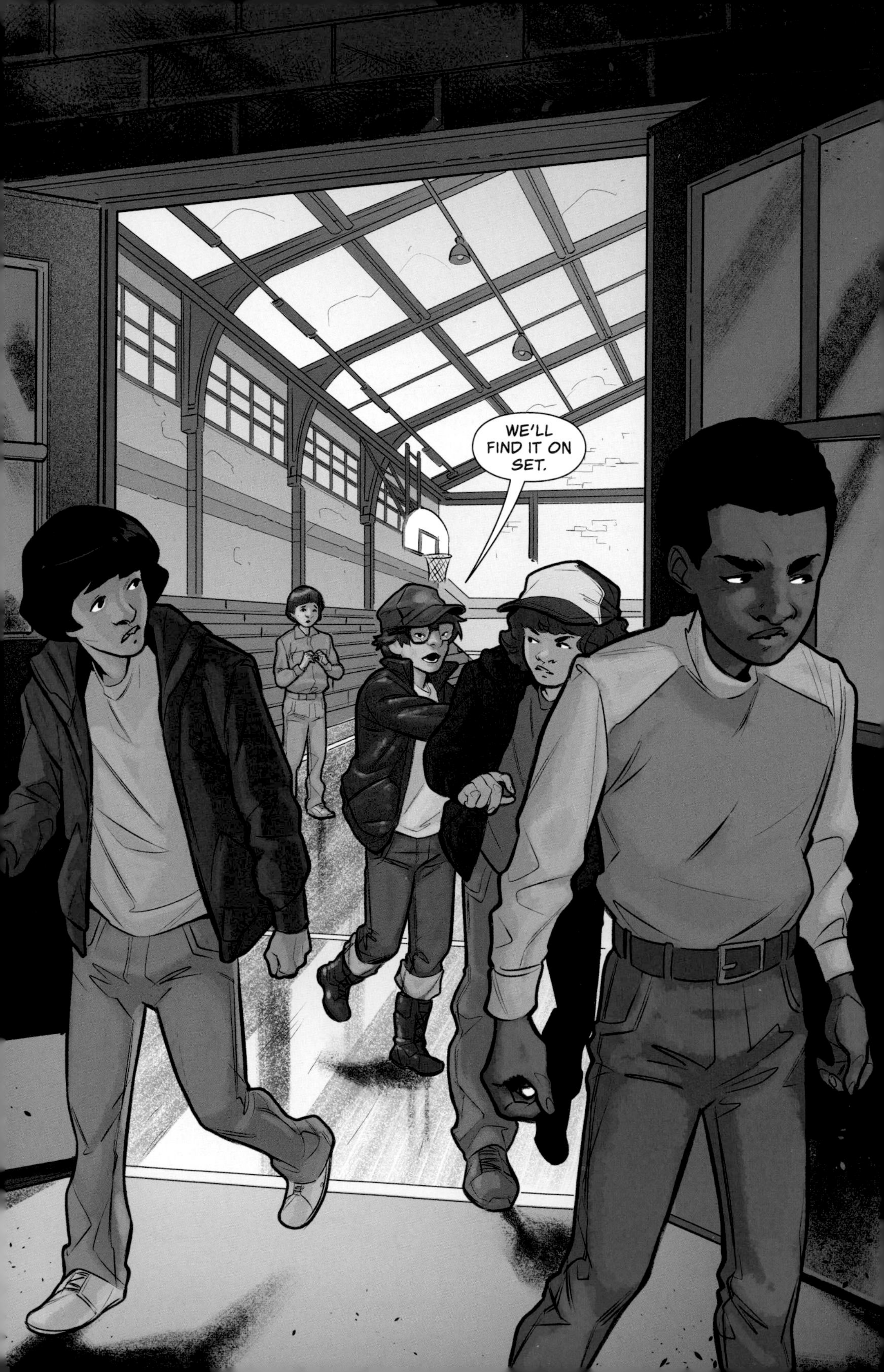
WE'LL FIND IT ON SET.

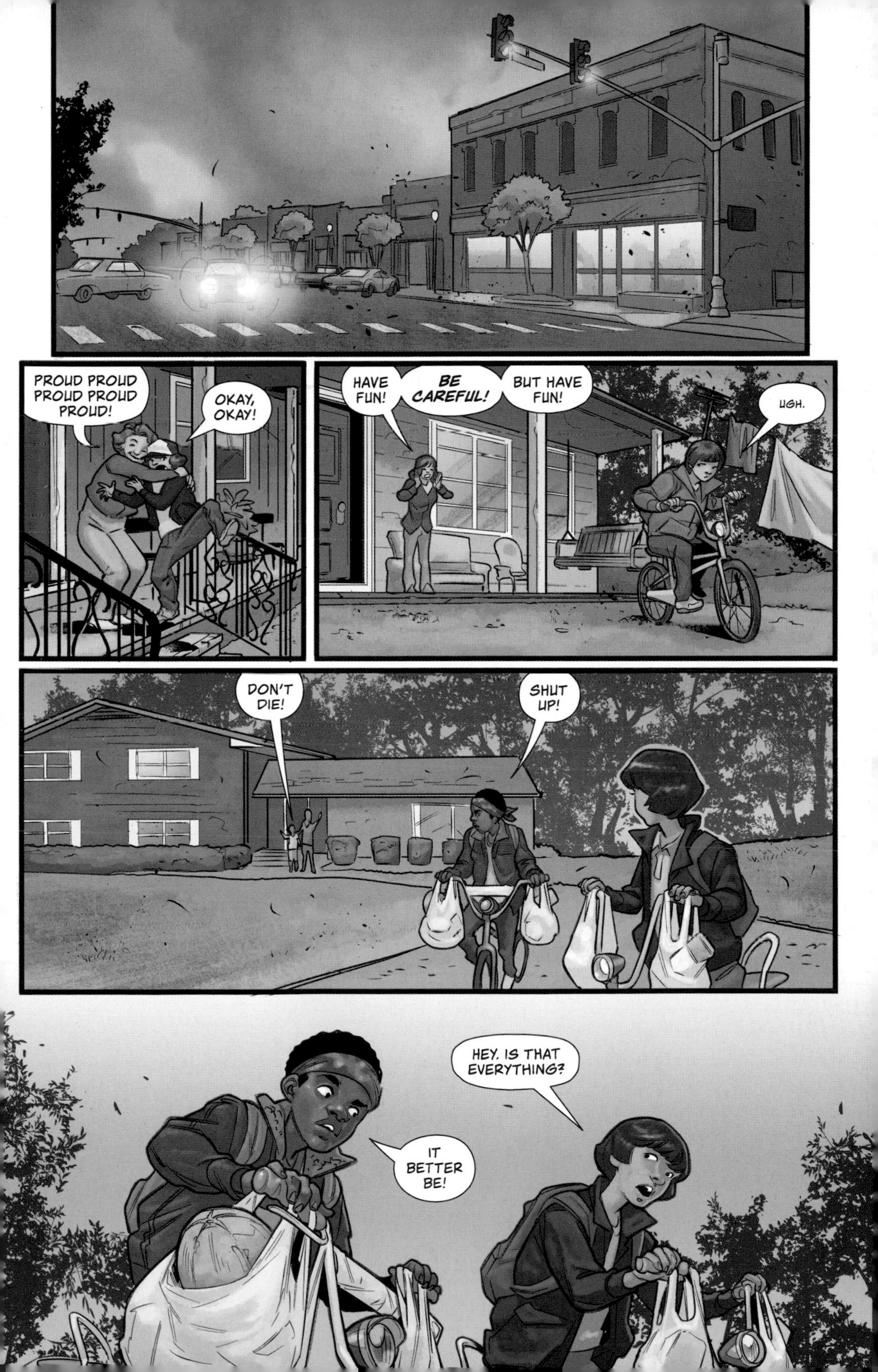
PROUD PROUD PROUD PROUD PROUD!
OKAY, OKAY!
HAVE FUN!
BE CAREFUL!
BUT HAVE FUN!
UGH.
DON'T DIE!
SHUT UP!
HEY. IS THAT EVERYTHING?
IT BETTER BE!

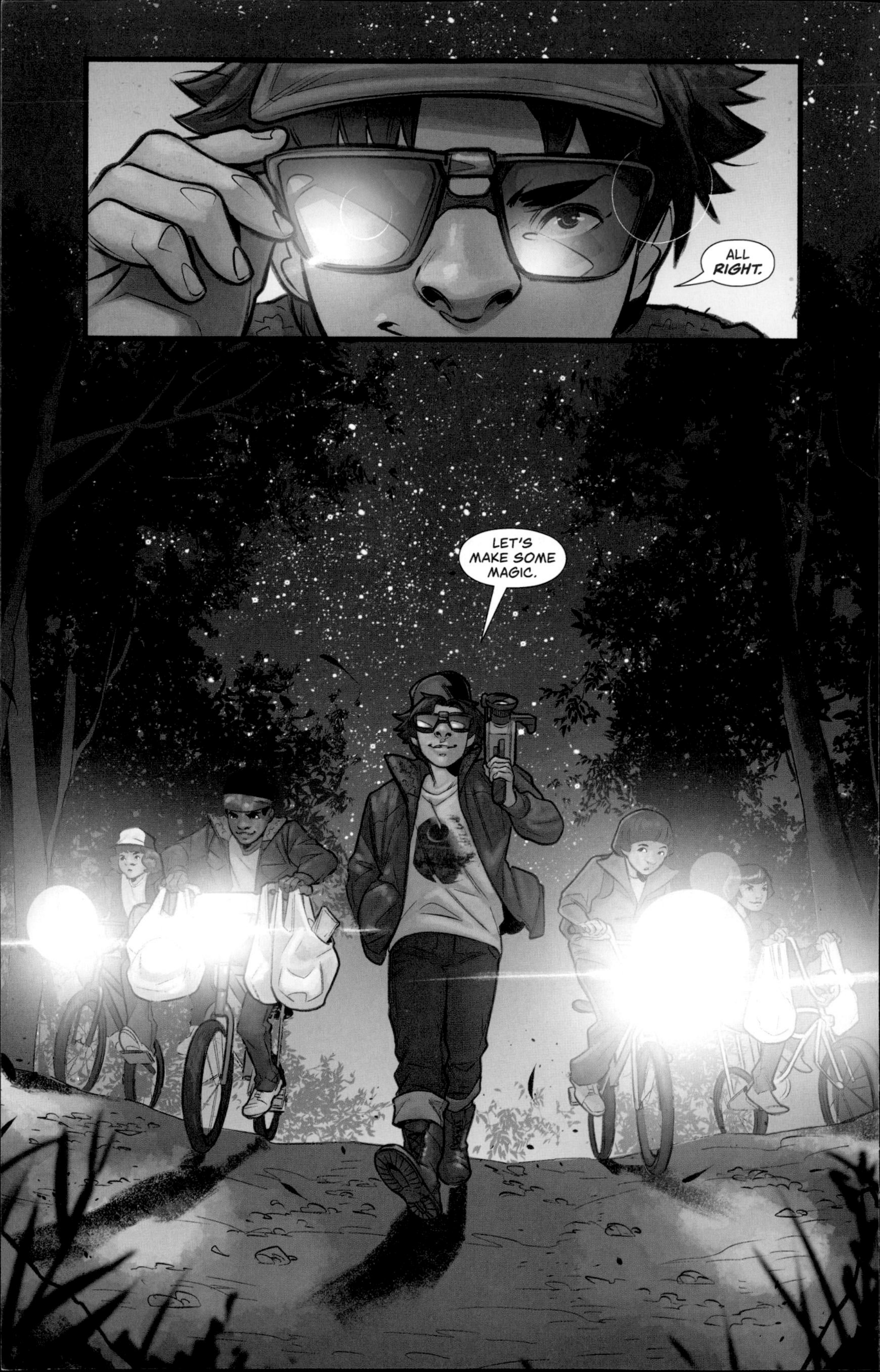
ALL RIGHT.
LET'S MAKE SOME MAGIC.

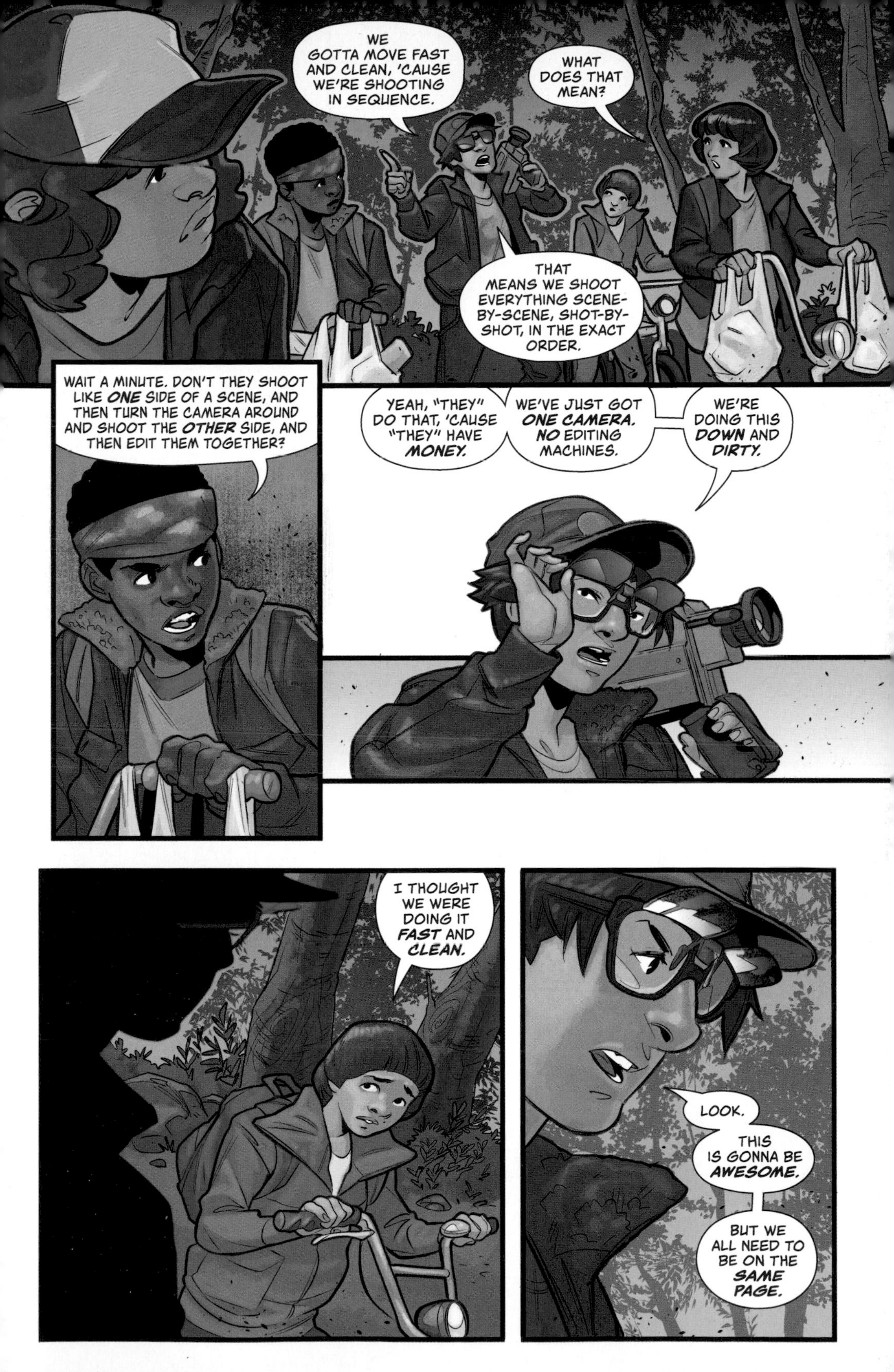
WE GOTTA MOVE FAST AND CLEAN, 'CAUSE WE'RE SHOOTING IN SEQUENCE.
WHAT DOES THAT MEAN?
THAT MEANS WE SHOOT EVERYTHING SCENE-BY-SCENE, SHOT-BY-SHOT, IN THE EXACT ORDER.
WAIT A MINUTE. DON'T THEY SHOOT LIKE *ONE* SIDE OF A SCENE, AND THEN TURN THE CAMERA AROUND AND SHOOT THE *OTHER* SIDE, AND THEN EDIT THEM TOGETHER?
YEAH, "THEY" DO THAT, 'CAUSE "THEY" HAVE *MONEY.*
WE'VE JUST GOT *ONE CAMERA. NO* EDITING MACHINES.
WE'RE DOING THIS *DOWN* AND *DIRTY.*
I THOUGHT WE WERE DOING IT *FAST* AND *CLEAN.*
LOOK.
THIS IS GONNA BE *AWESOME.*
BUT WE ALL NEED TO BE ON THE *SAME PAGE.*

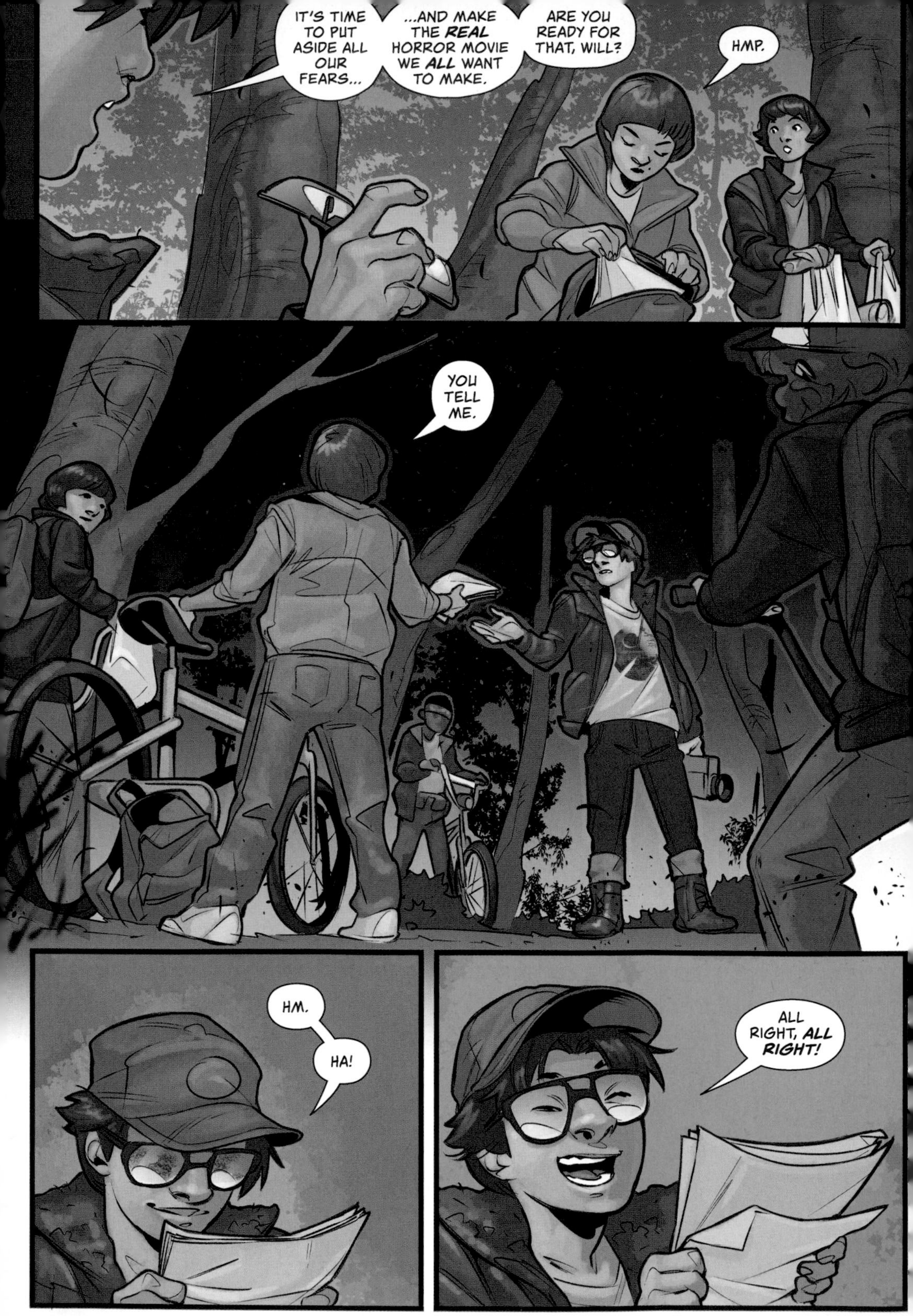
IT'S TIME TO PUT ASIDE ALL OUR FEARS...
...AND MAKE THE REAL HORROR MOVIE WE ALL WANT TO MAKE.
ARE YOU READY FOR THAT, WILL?
HMP.
YOU TELL ME.
HM.
HA!
ALL RIGHT, ALL RIGHT!

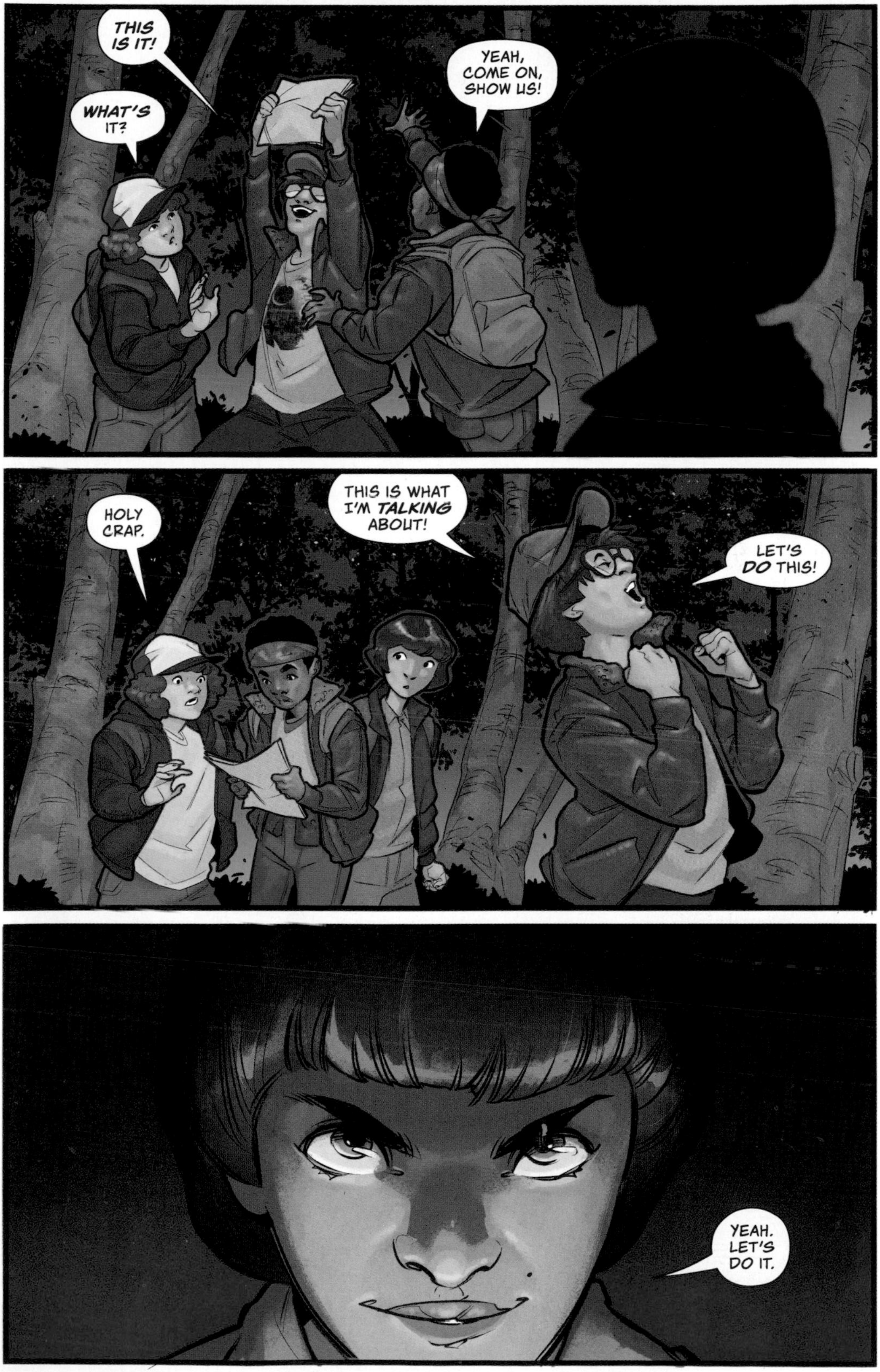
THIS IS IT!
WHAT'S IT?
YEAH, COME ON, SHOW US!
HOLY CRAP.
THIS IS WHAT I'M TALKING ABOUT!
LET'S DO THIS!
YEAH. LET'S DO IT.

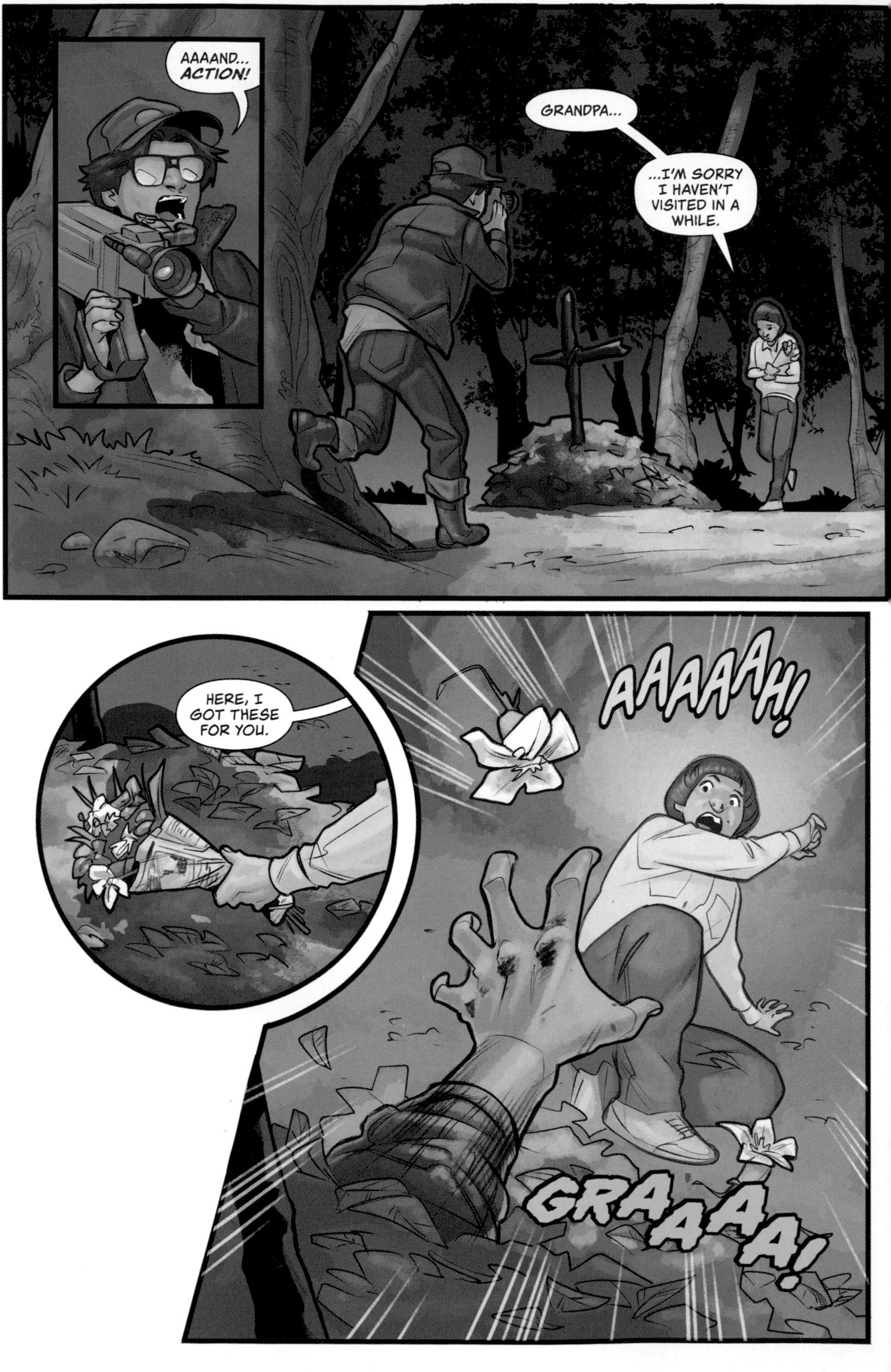
AAAAND... ACTION!
GRANDPA...
...I'M SORRY I HAVEN'T VISITED IN A WHILE.
HERE, I GOT THESE FOR YOU.
AAAAAH!
GRAAAAA!

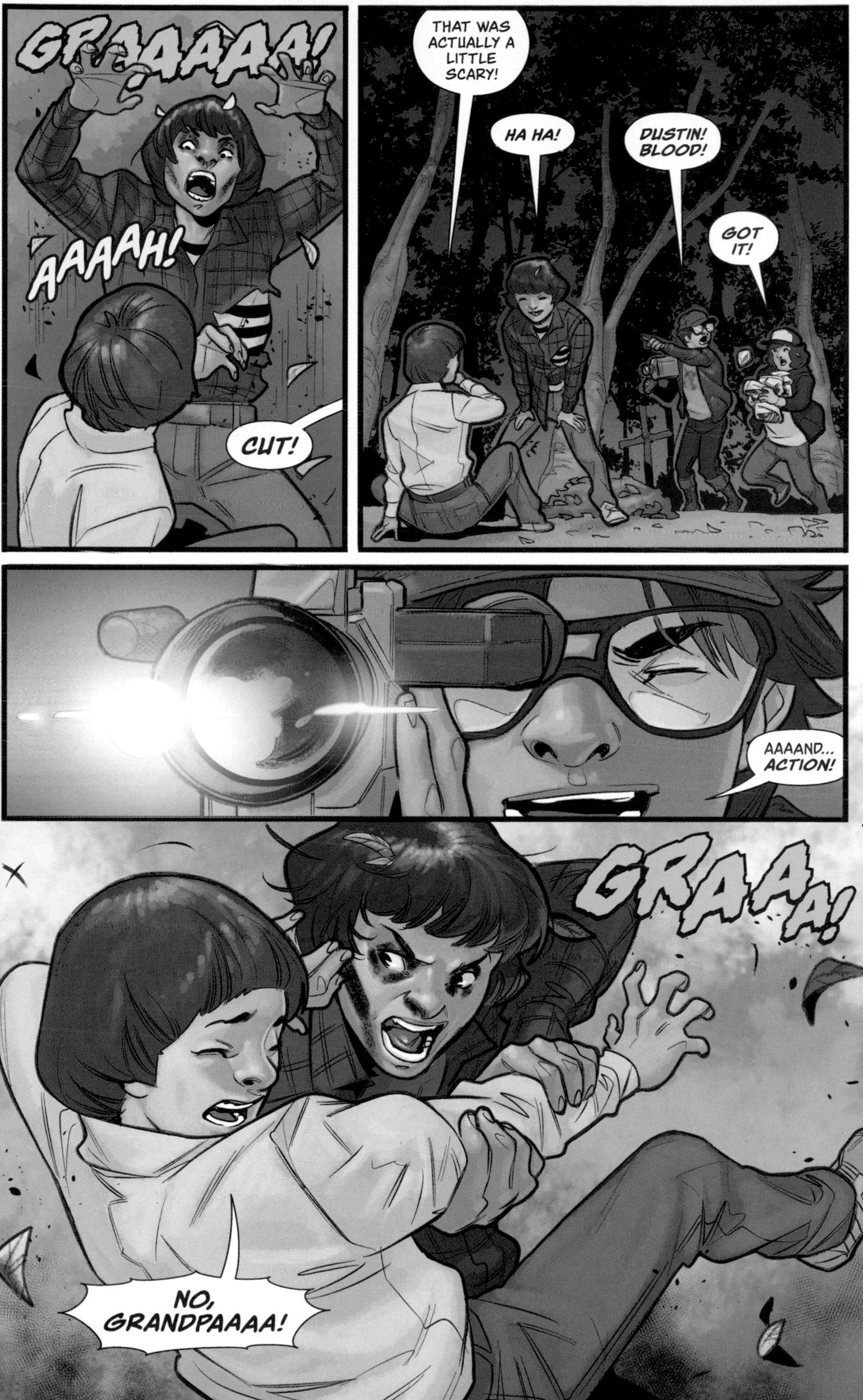
GRAAAAA!
AAAAH!
CUT!
THAT WAS ACTUALLY A LITTLE SCARY!
HA HA!
DUSTIN! BLOOD!
GOT IT!
AAAAND... ACTION!
GRAAAA!
NO, GRANDPAAAA!

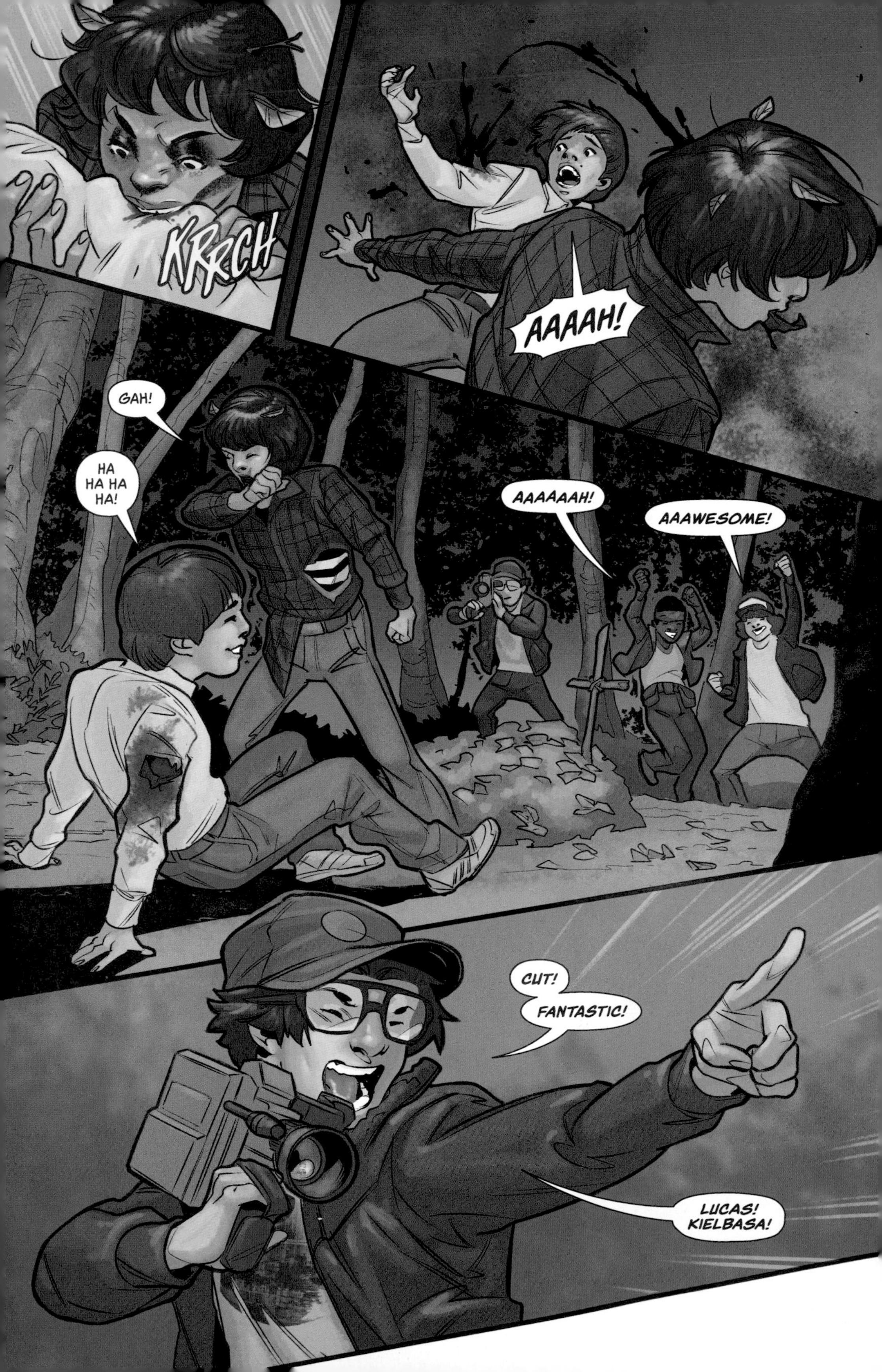
KRRCH
AAAAH!
GAH!
HA HA HA HA!
AAAAAAH!
AAAWESOME!
CUT!
FANTASTIC!
LUCAS! KIELBASA!

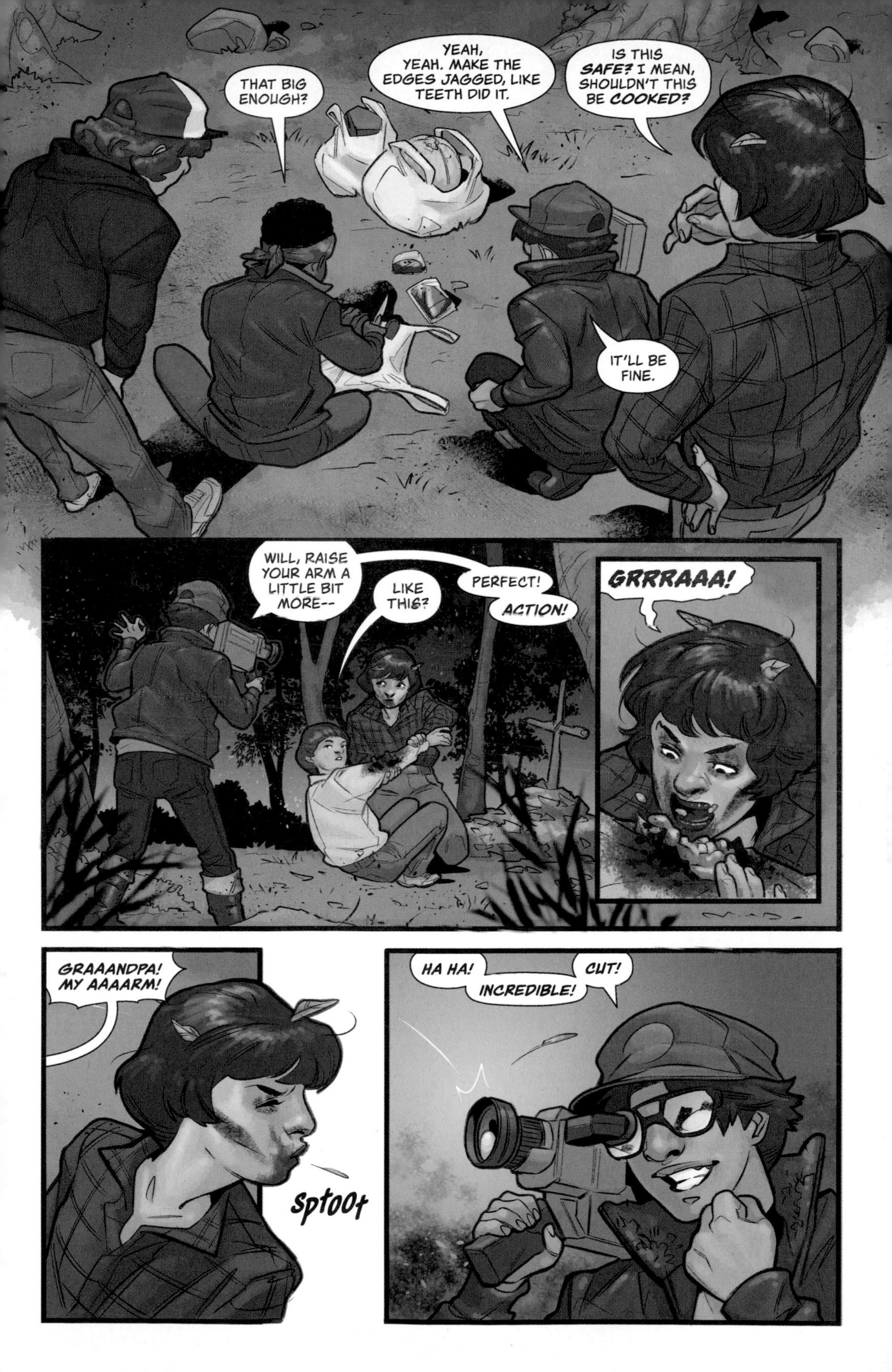
THAT BIG ENOUGH?
YEAH, YEAH. MAKE THE EDGES JAGGED, LIKE TEETH DID IT.
IS THIS SAFE? I MEAN, SHOULDN'T THIS BE COOKED?
IT'LL BE FINE.
WILL, RAISE YOUR ARM A LITTLE BIT MORE--
LIKE THIS?
PERFECT!
ACTION!
GRRRAAA!
GRAAANDPA! MY AAAARM!
SPTOOT
HA HA!
INCREDIBLE!
CUT!

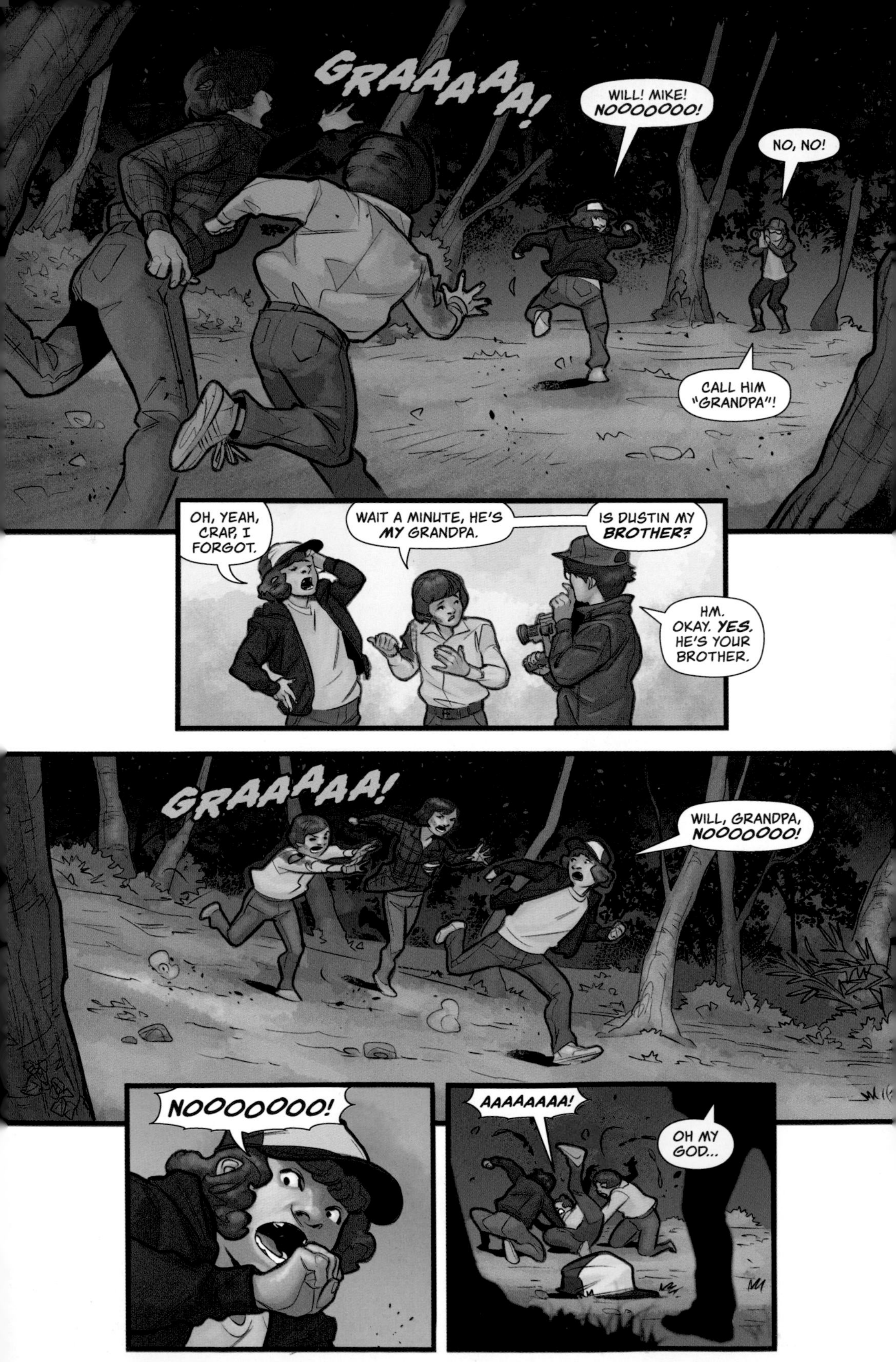
GRAAAAAA!
WILL! MIKE! NOOOOOOO!
NO, NO!
CALL HIM "GRANDPA"!
OH, YEAH, CRAP, I FORGOT.
WAIT A MINUTE, HE'S MY GRANDPA.
IS DUSTIN MY BROTHER?
HM. OKAY. YES. HE'S YOUR BROTHER.
GRAAAAAA!
WILL, GRANDPA, NOOOOOOO!
NOOOOOOO!
AAAAAAAA!
OH MY GOD...

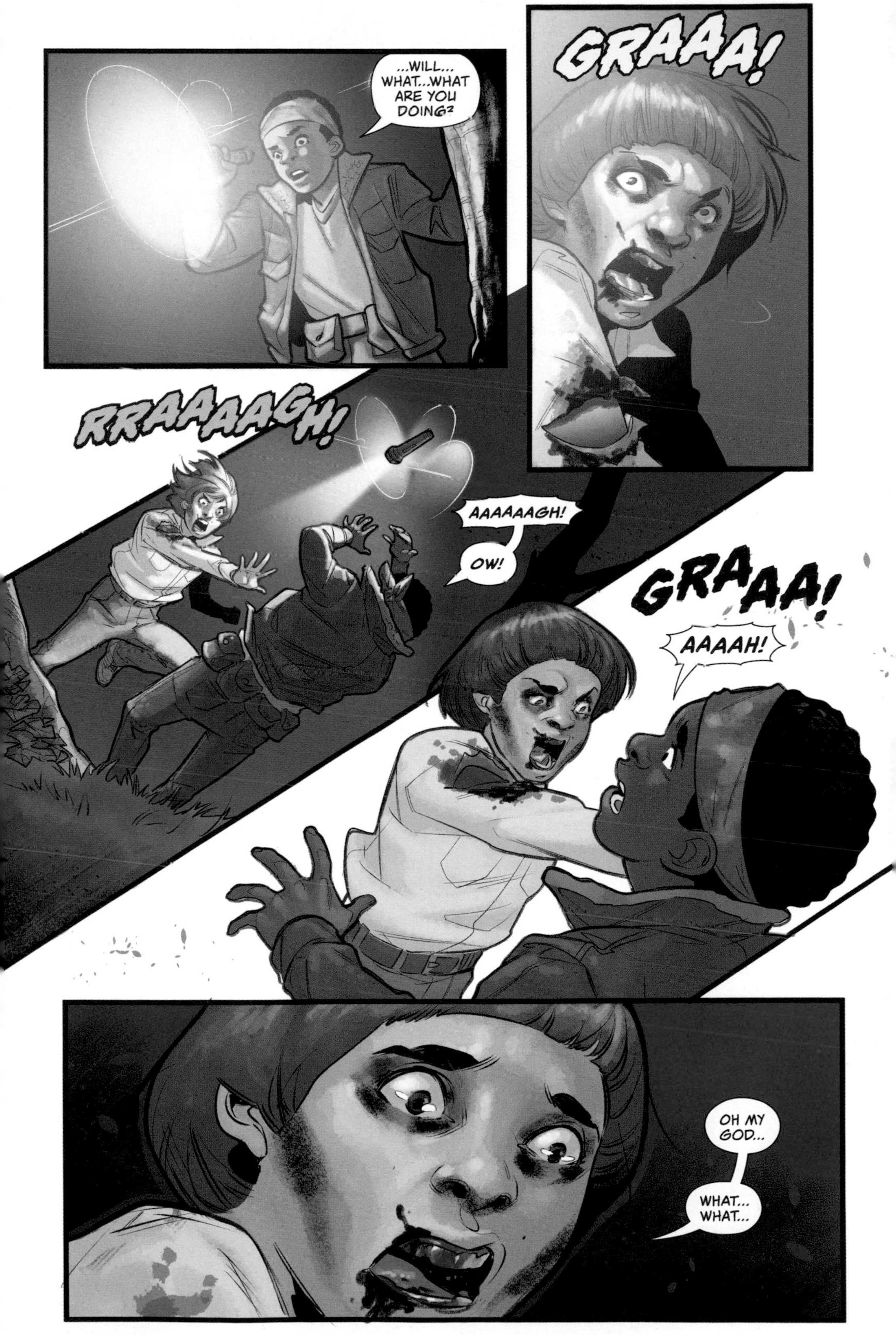
...WILL... WHAT...WHAT ARE YOU DOING?
GRAAA!
RRAAAAAGH!
AAAAAAGH!
OW!
GRAAAA!
AAAAH!
OH MY GOD...
WHAT... WHAT...

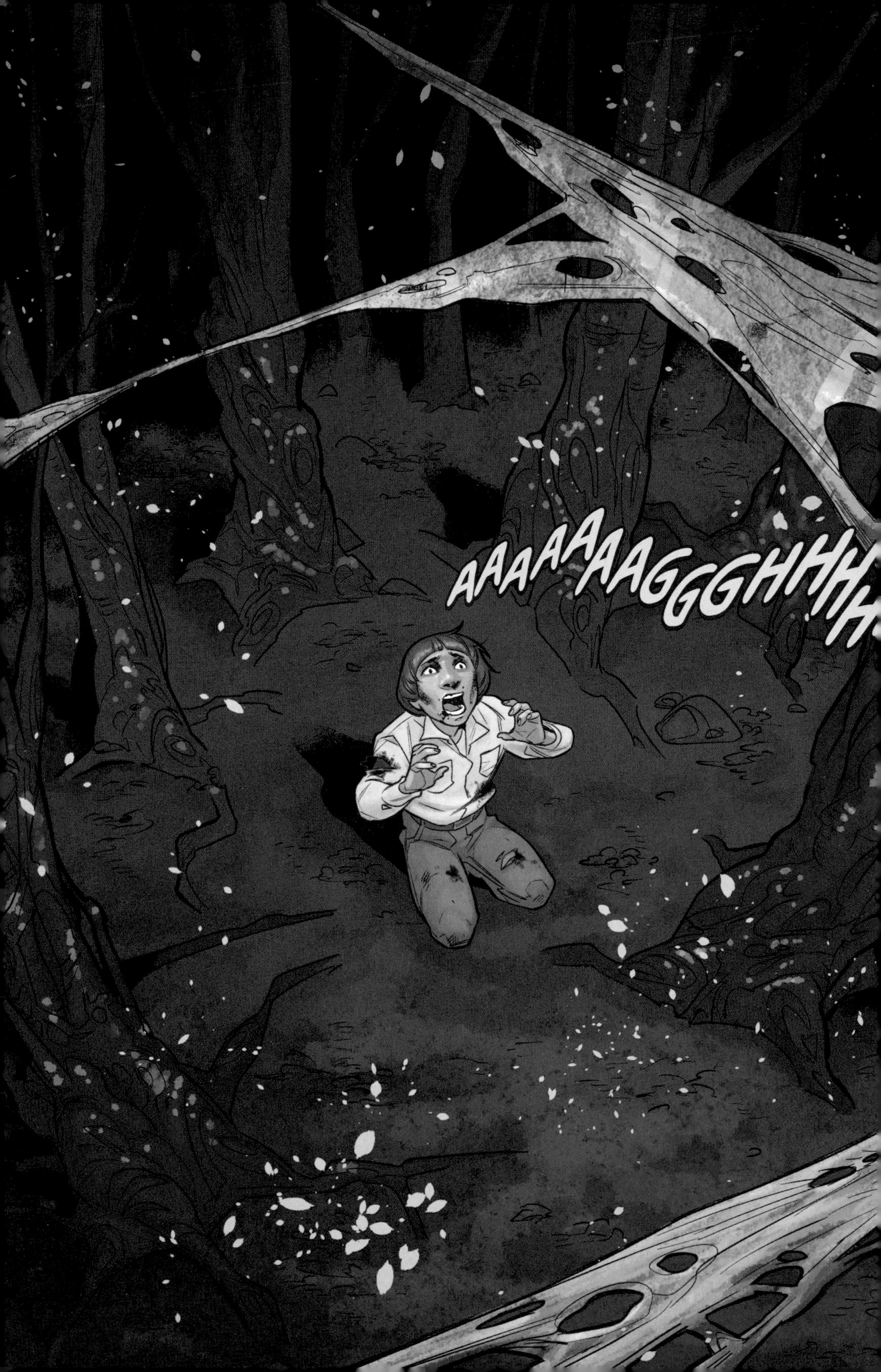
AAAAAAAGGGHHHH

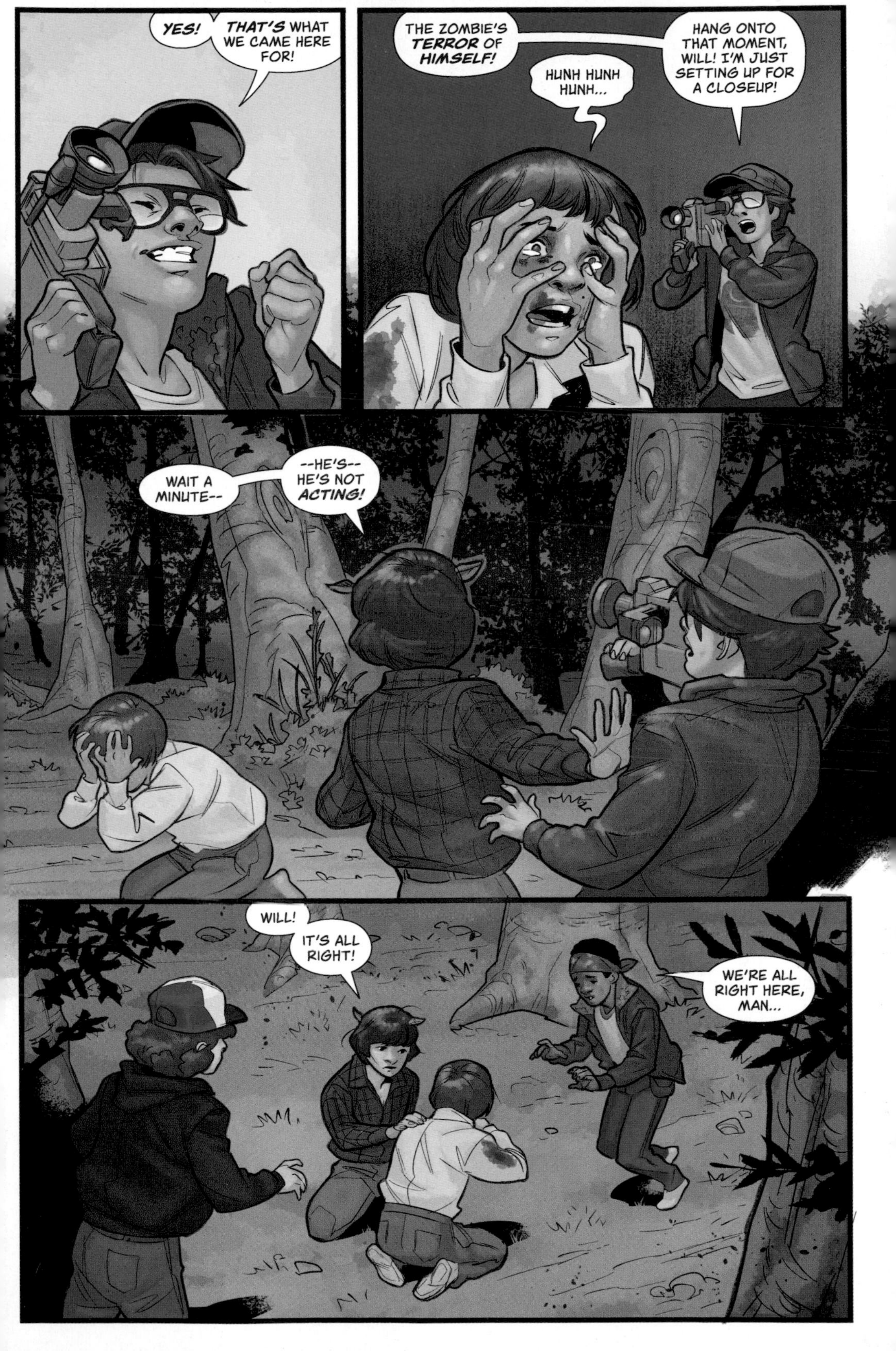

YES!
THAT'S WHAT WE CAME HERE FOR!
THE ZOMBIE'S TERROR OF HIMSELF!
HANG ONTO THAT MOMENT, WILL! I'M JUST SETTING UP FOR A CLOSEUP!
HUNH HUNH HUNH...
WAIT A MINUTE--
--HE'S-- HE'S NOT ACTING!
WILL!
IT'S ALL RIGHT!
WE'RE ALL RIGHT HERE, MAN...

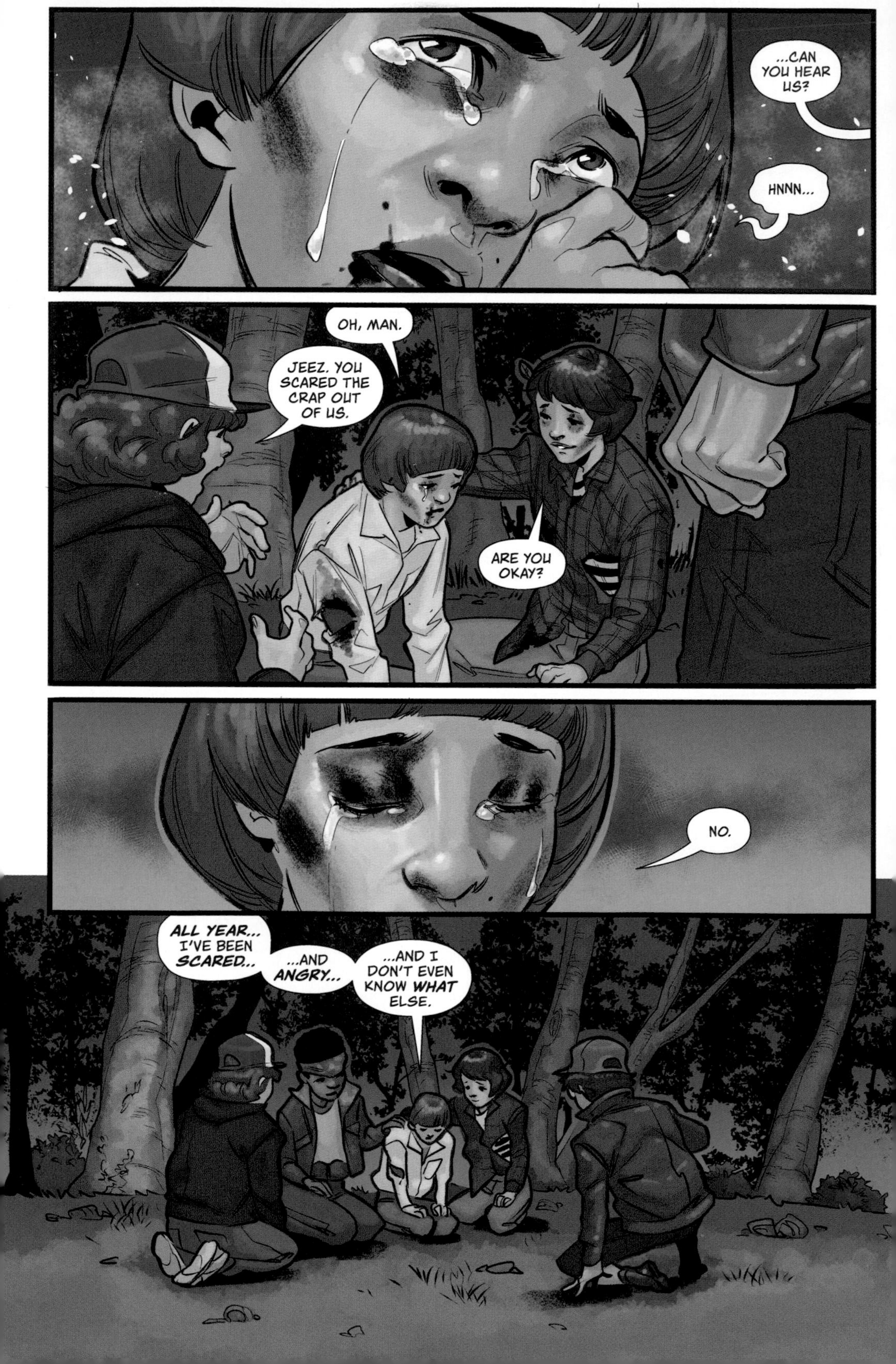
...CAN YOU HEAR US?
HNNN...
OH, MAN.
JEEZ. YOU SCARED THE CRAP OUT OF US.
ARE YOU OKAY?
NO.
ALL YEAR... I'VE BEEN SCARED...
...AND ANGRY...
...AND I DON'T EVEN KNOW WHAT ELSE.

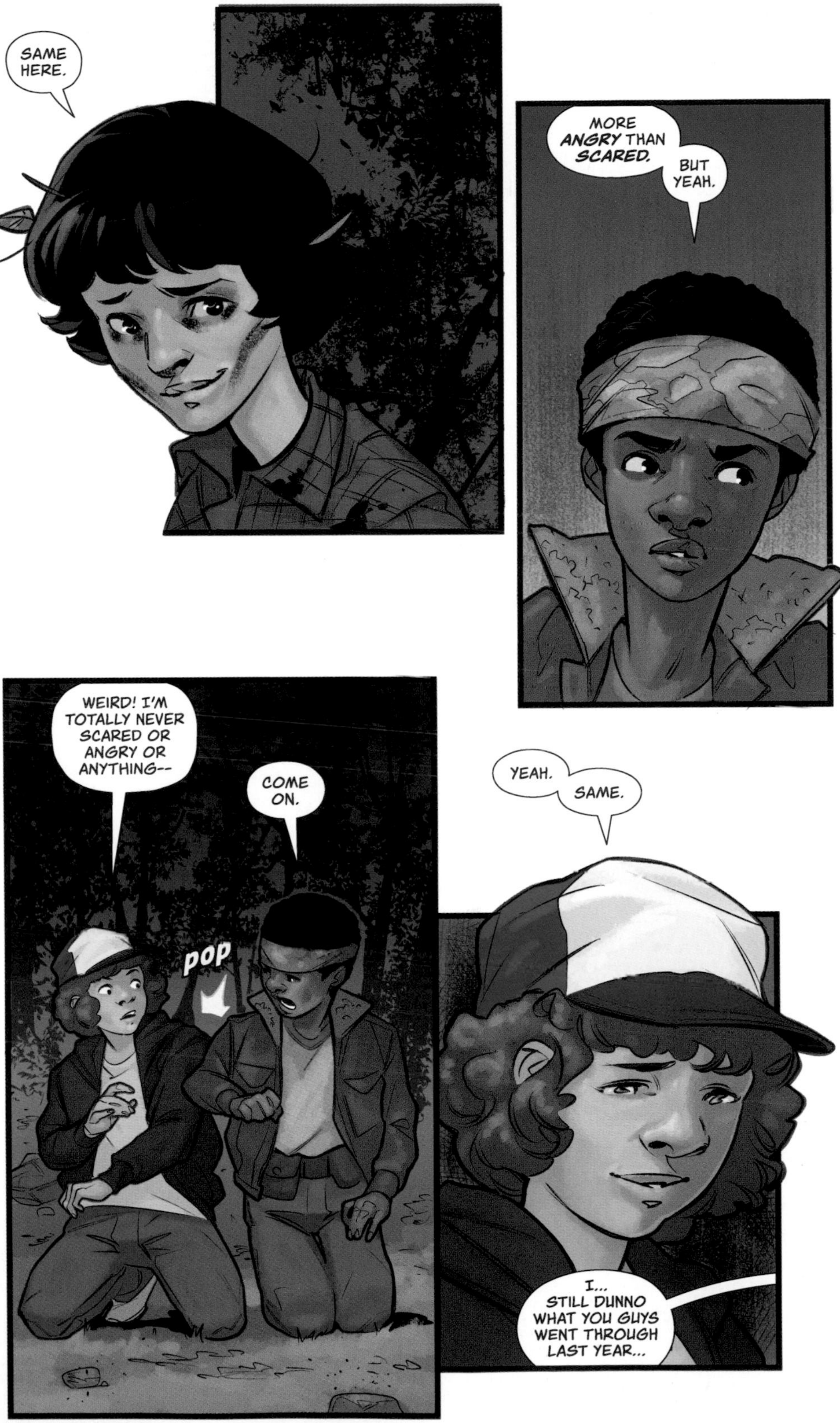
SAME HERE.
MORE ANGRY THAN SCARED.
BUT YEAH.
WEIRD! I'M TOTALLY NEVER SCARED OR ANGRY OR ANYTHING--
COME ON.
POP
YEAH.
SAME.
I... STILL DUNNO WHAT YOU GUYS WENT THROUGH LAST YEAR...

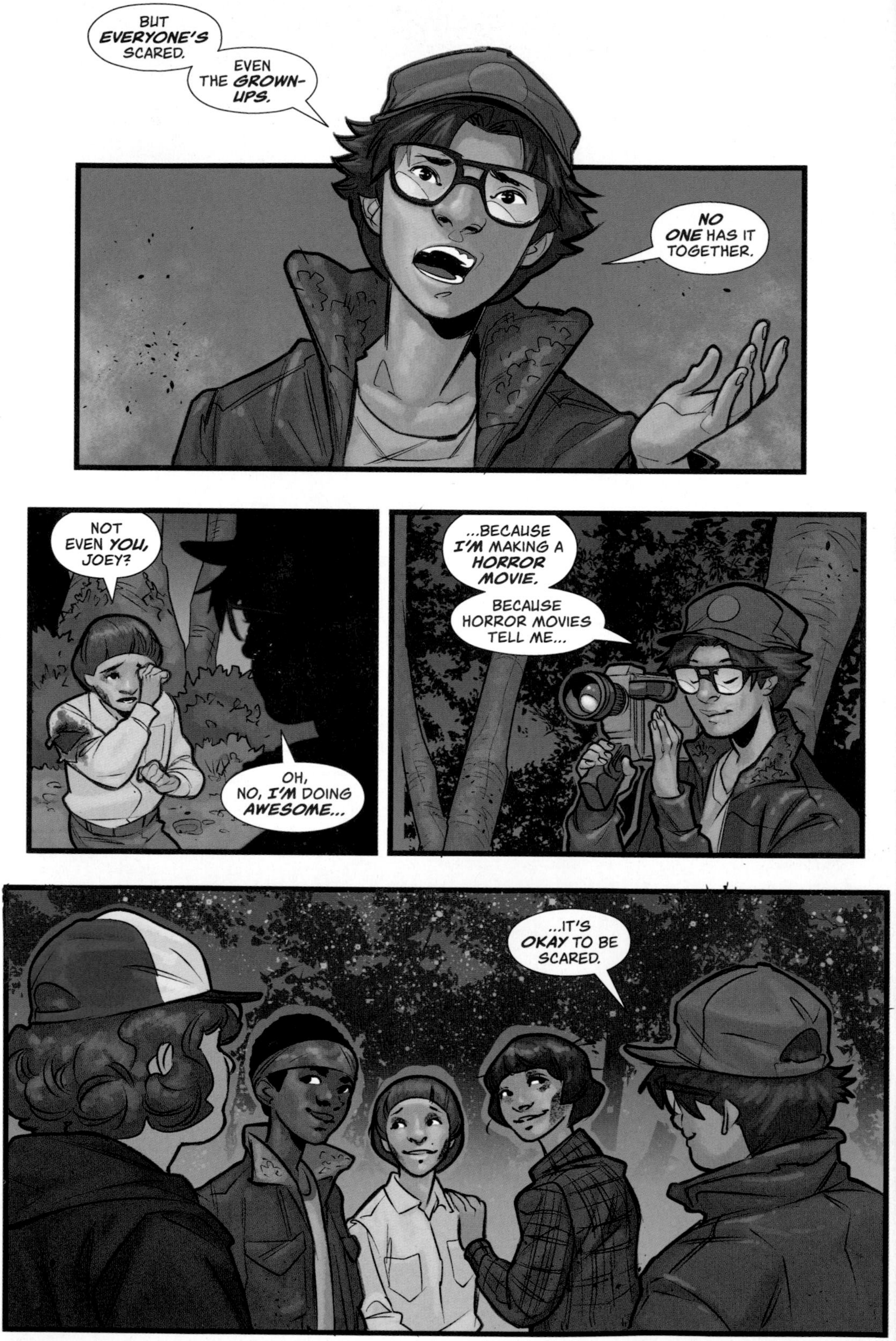
BUT EVERYONE'S SCARED.
EVEN THE GROWN-UPS.
NO ONE HAS IT TOGETHER.
NOT EVEN YOU, JOEY?
OH, NO, I'M DOING AWESOME...
...BECAUSE I'M MAKING A HORROR MOVIE.
BECAUSE HORROR MOVIES TELL ME...
...IT'S OKAY TO BE SCARED.

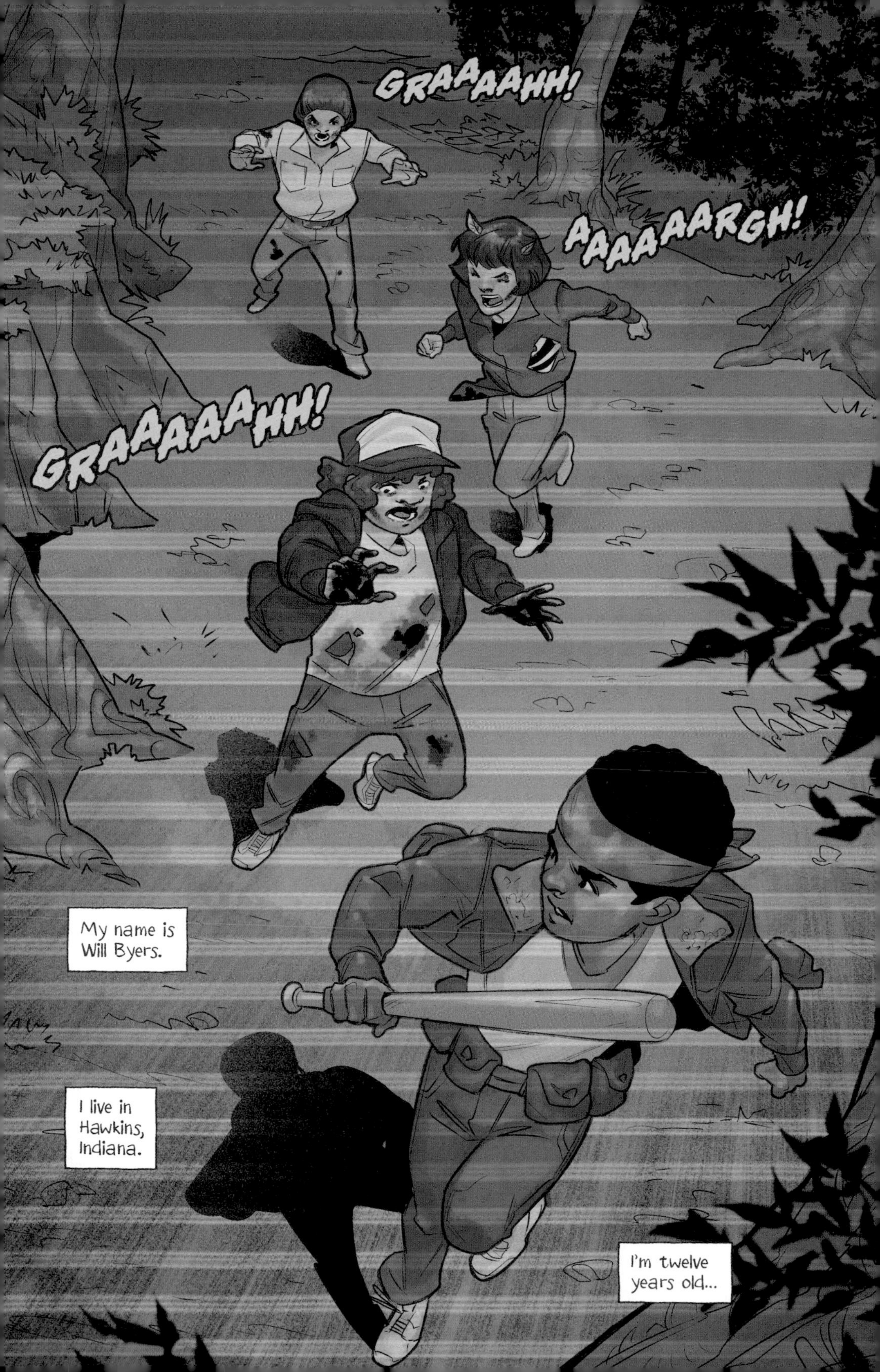
GRAAAAHH!
AAAAAARGH!
GRAAAAAHH!
My name is Will Byers.
I live in Hawkins, Indiana.
I'm twelve years old...

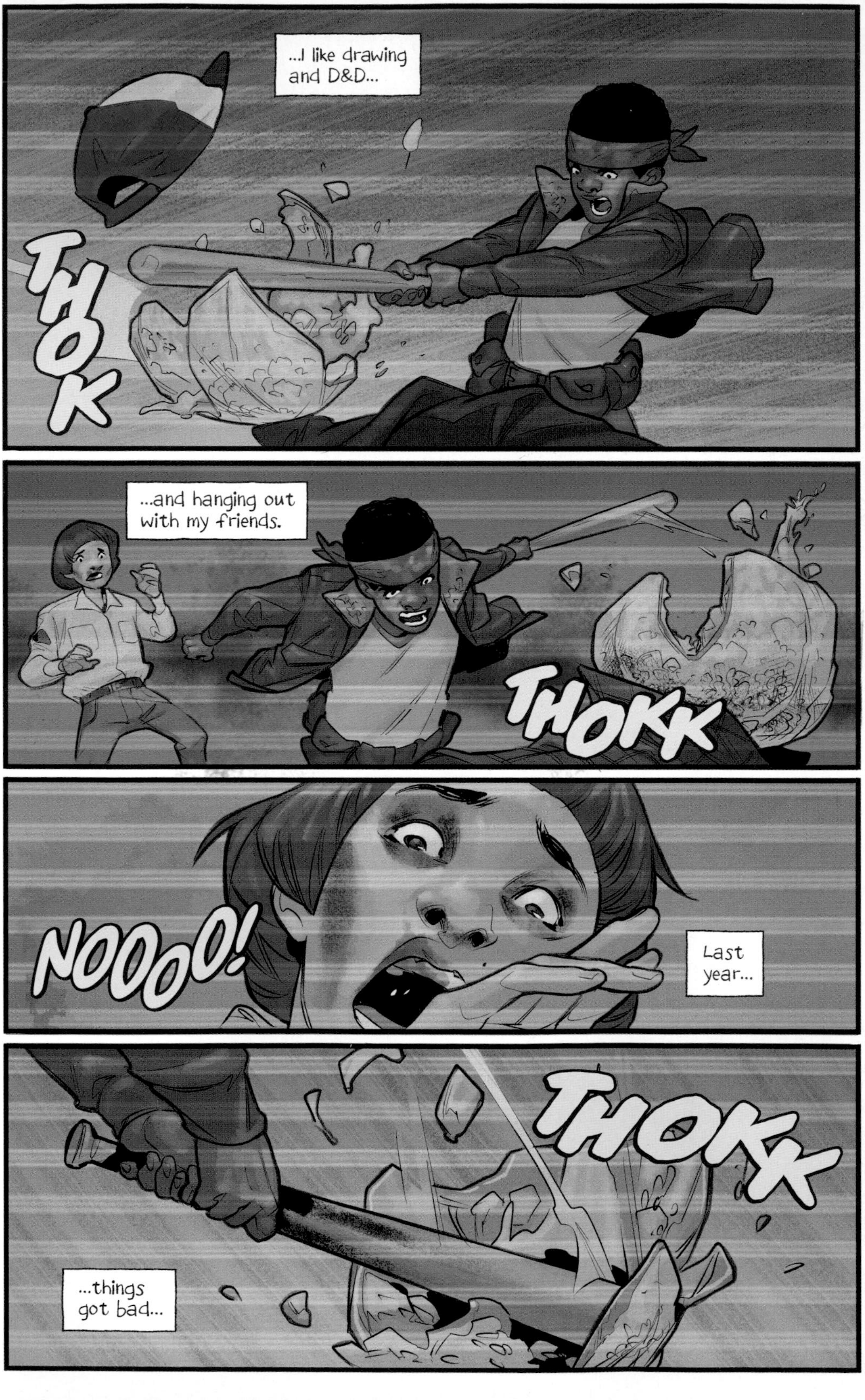
...I like drawing and D&D...
THOK
...and hanging out with my friends.
THOKK
NOOOOO!
Last year...
THOKK
...things got bad...

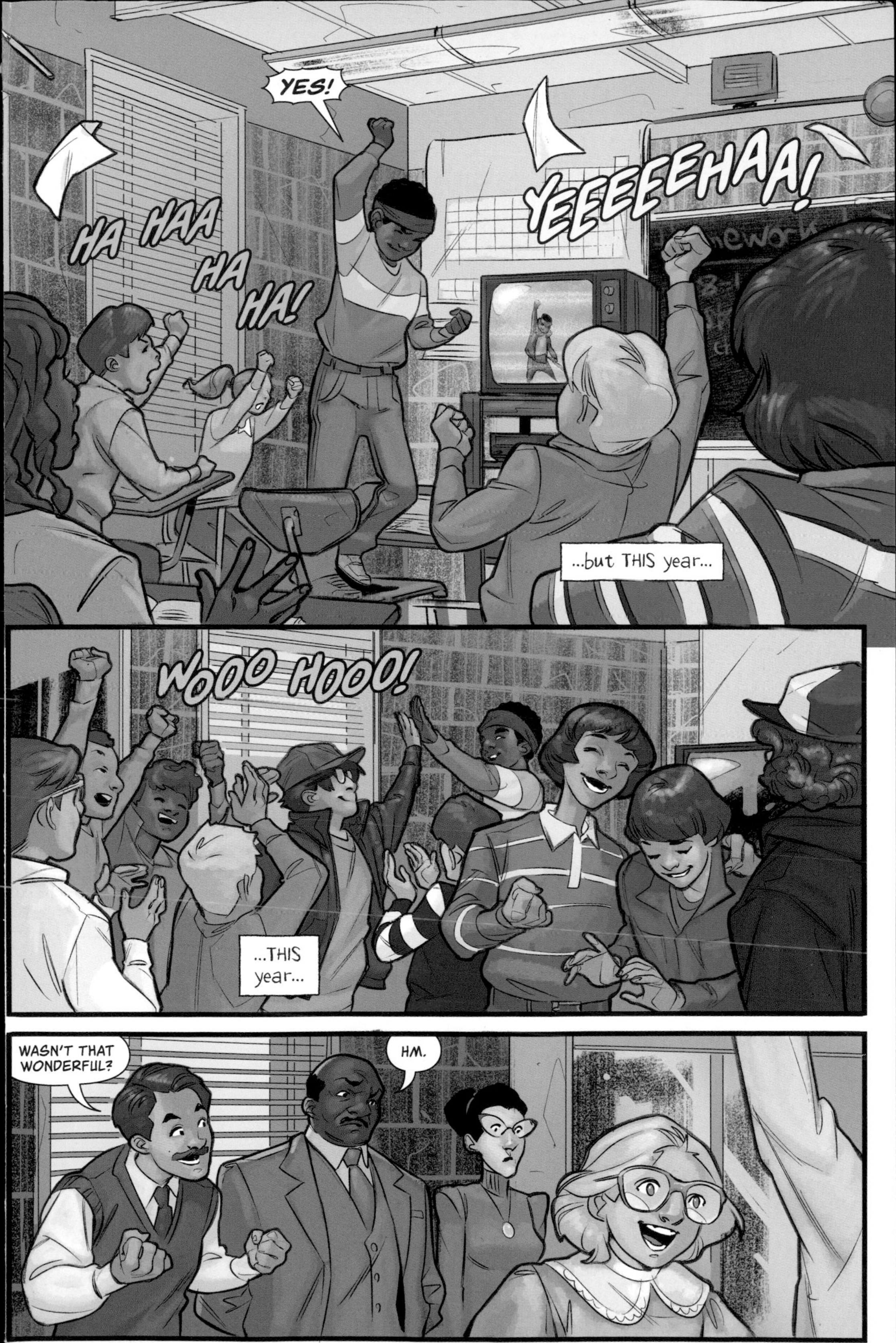
YES!
HA HAA HA HA!
YEEEEEHAA!
...but THIS year...
WOOO HOOO!
...THIS year...
WASN'T THAT WONDERFUL?
HM.

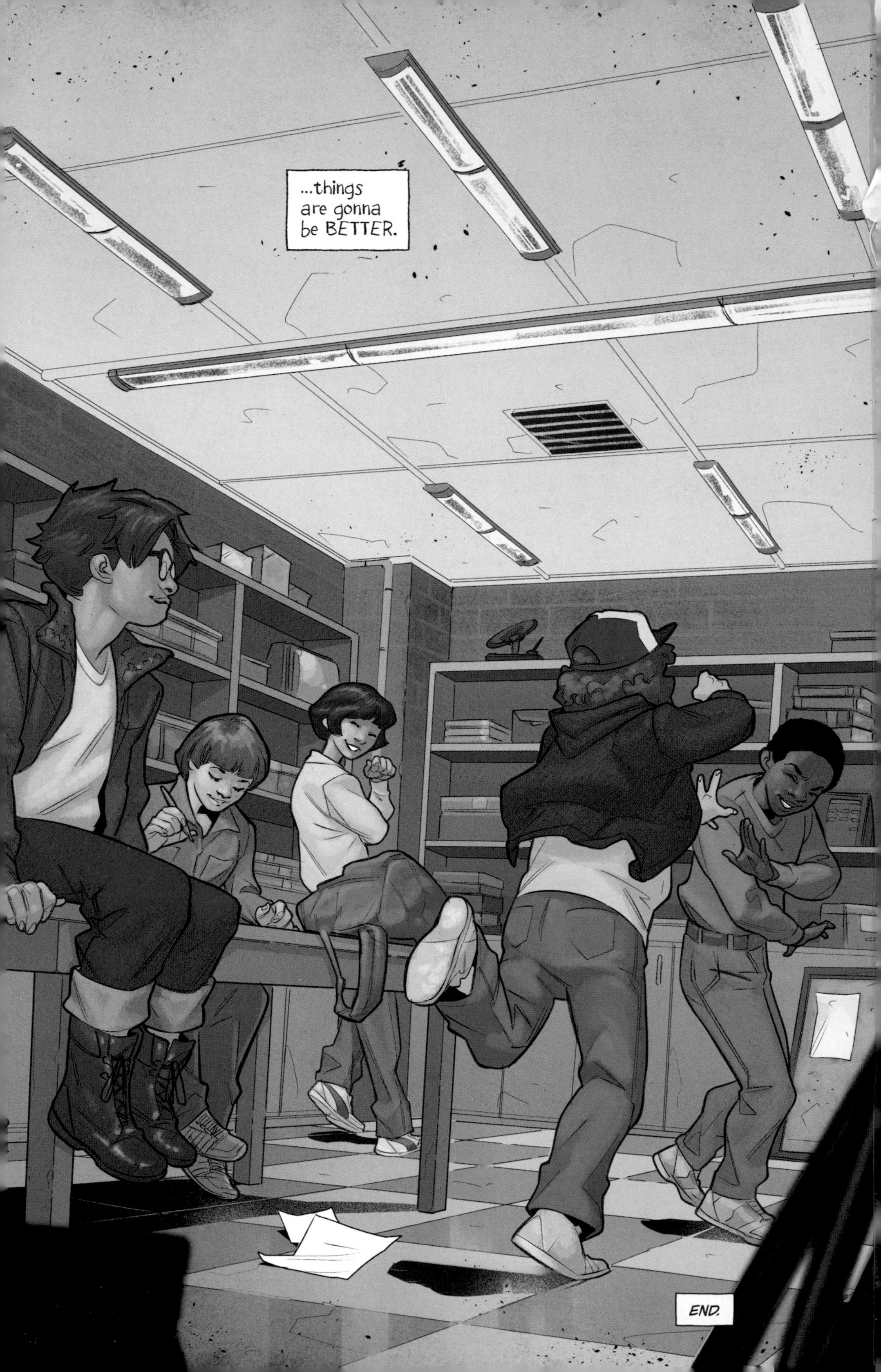
...things are gonna be BETTER.
END.